THIS COMIC BELONGS TO:

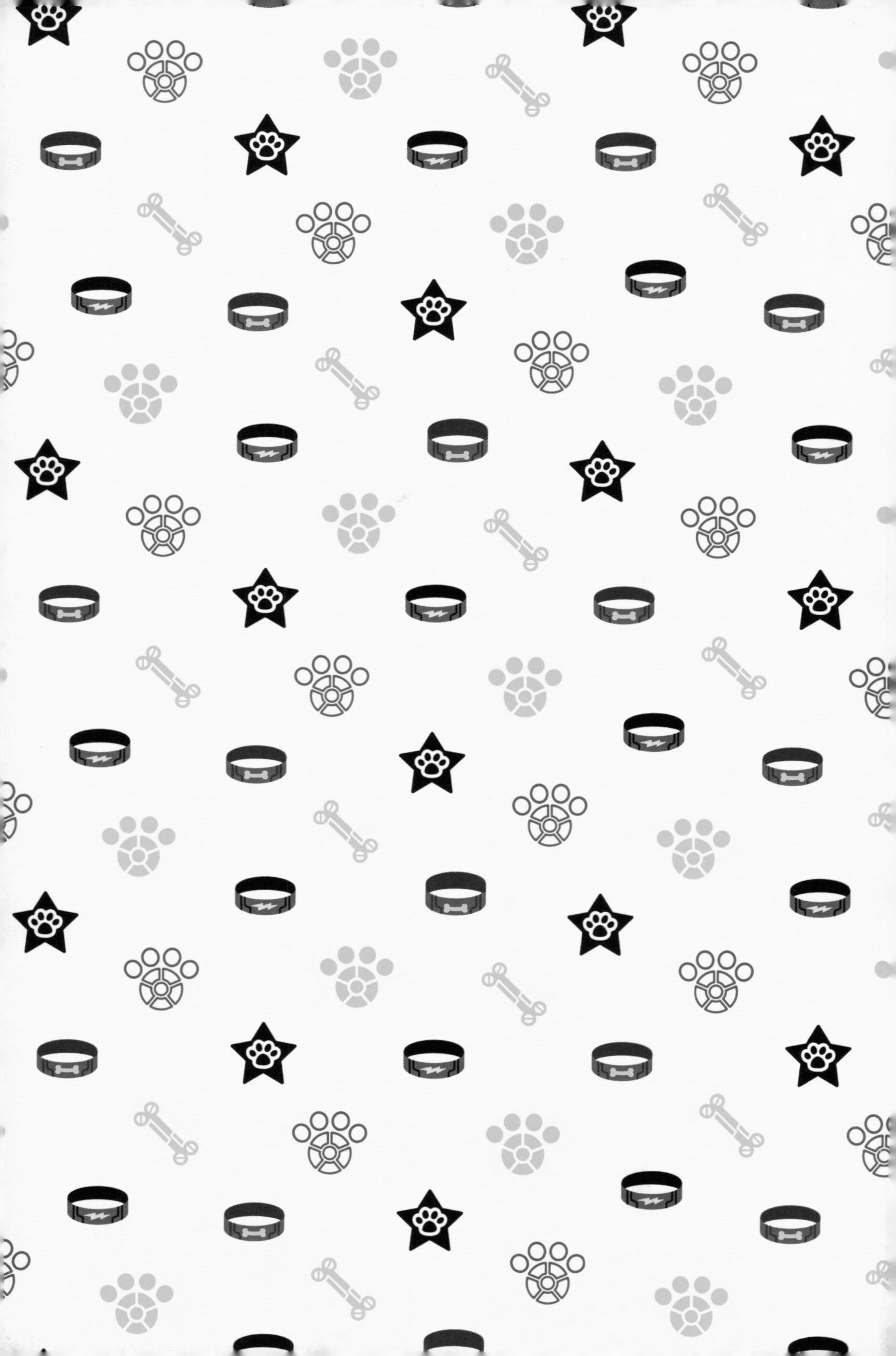

Disney

PUPPY DOG PALS

Published simultaneously in the United States and Canada by Joe Books Ltd,
489 College Street, Suite 203, Toronto, ON M6G 1A5.

www.joebooks.com

Hardcover and paperback published simultaneously: March 2018

Hardcover ISBN: 978-1-77275-674-6
Paperback ISBN: 978-1-77275-869-6
ebook ISBN: 978-1-77275-864-1

Library and Archives Canada Cataloguing in Publication
information is available upon request.

Printed and bound in Canada
3 5 7 9 10 8 6 4 2

DISNEP PUPPY DOG PALS

THEIR ROYAL PUG-NESS

CINESTORY COMIC

JOE BOOKS LTD

MEET THE PUPPY DOG PALS AND THEIR FAMILY!

ROLLY
is Bingo's younger brother. He's silly and sweet.

BINGO
is Rolly's older brother. He always has a plan!

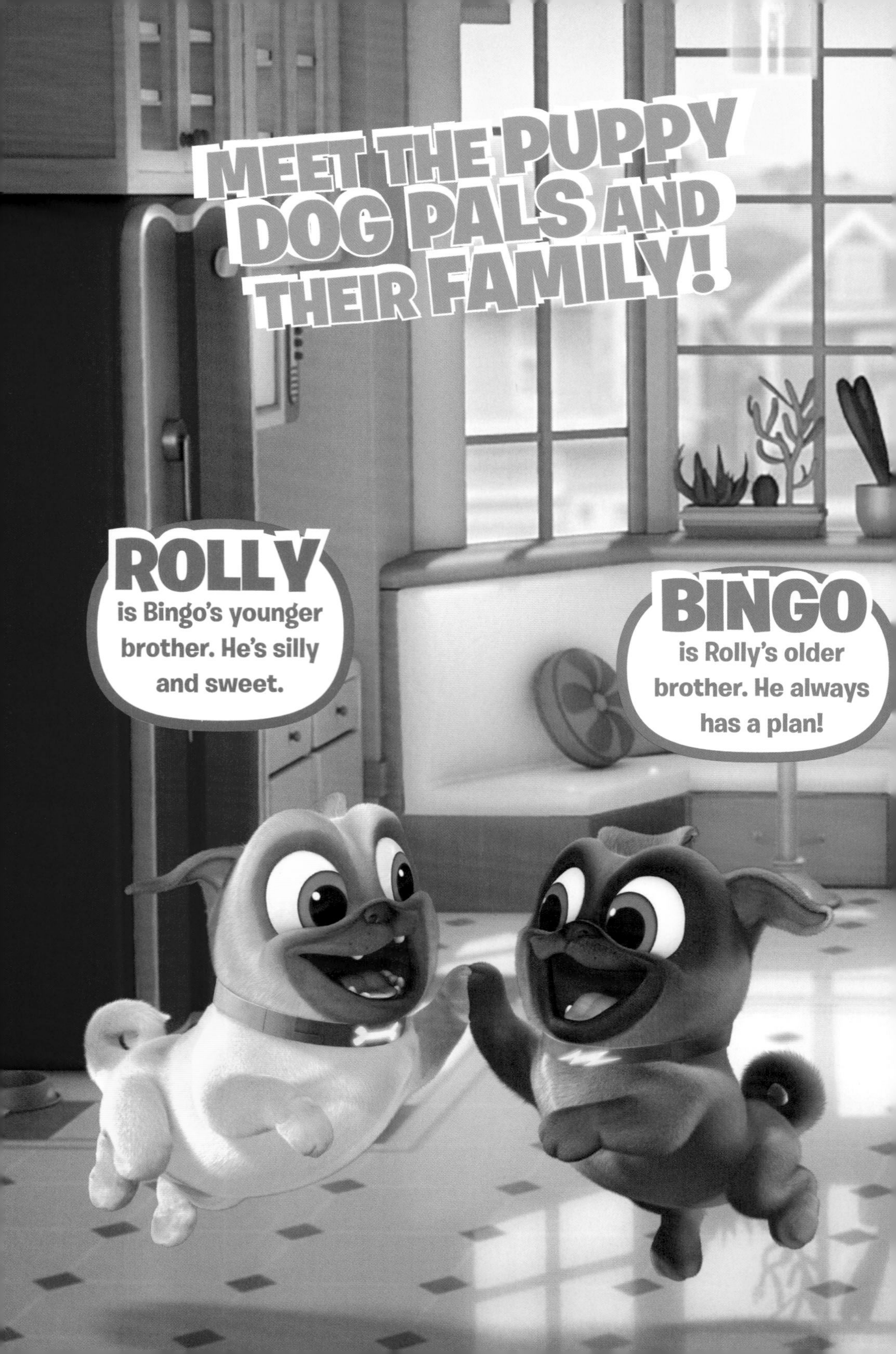

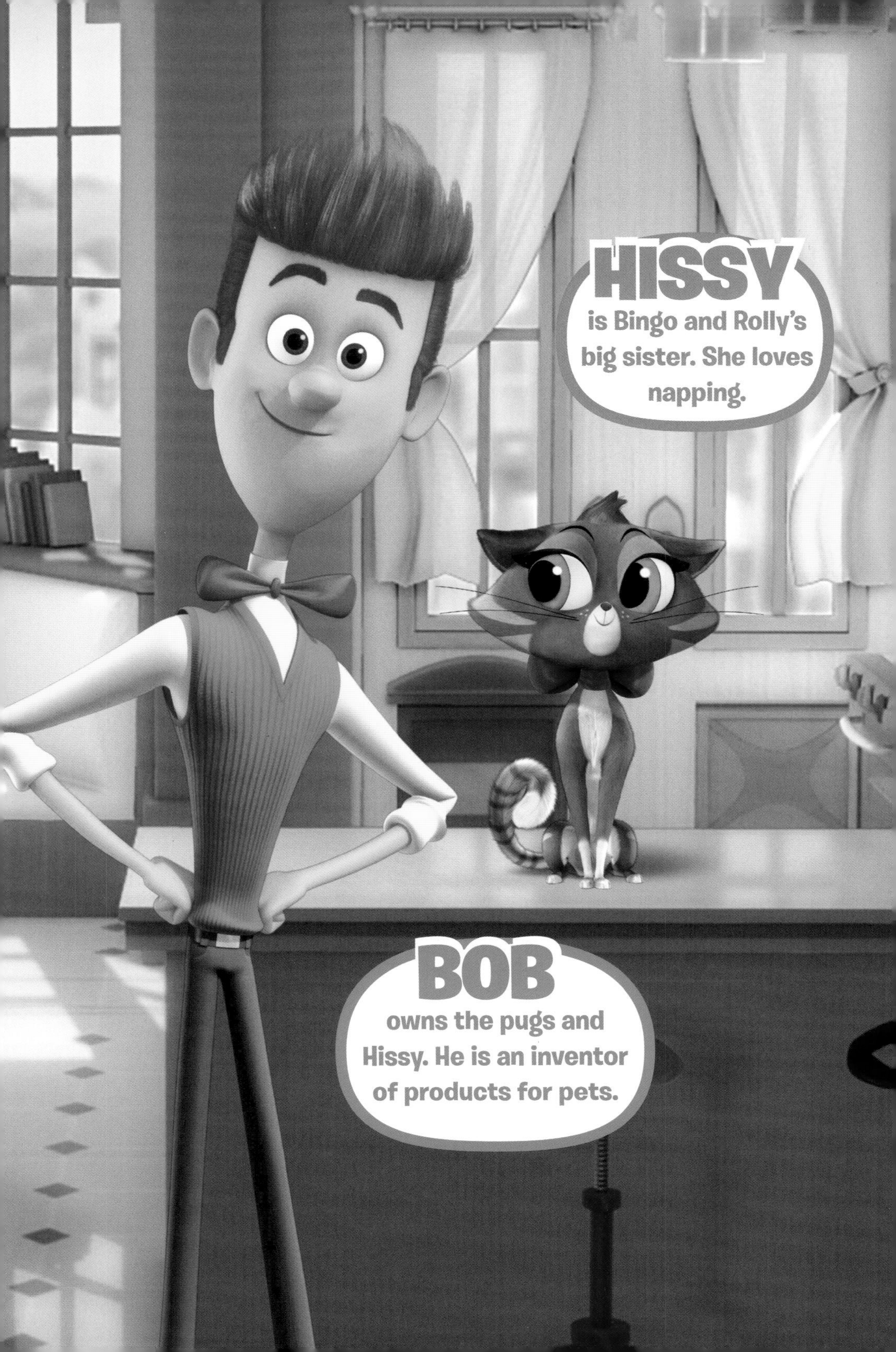

HISSY
is Bingo and Rolly's big sister. She loves napping.

BOB
owns the pugs and Hissy. He is an inventor of products for pets.

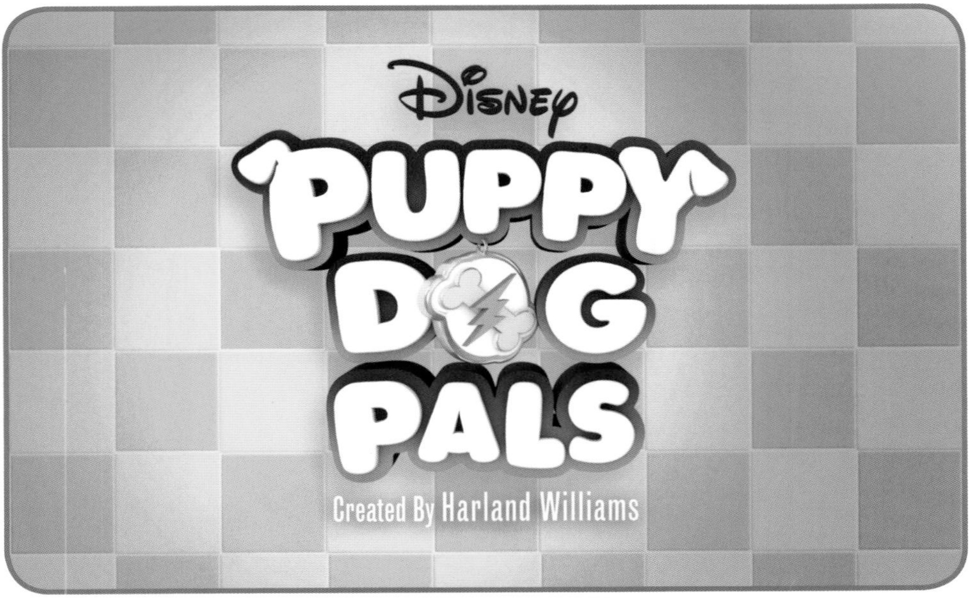
DISNEY
PUPPY DOG PALS
Created By Harland Williams

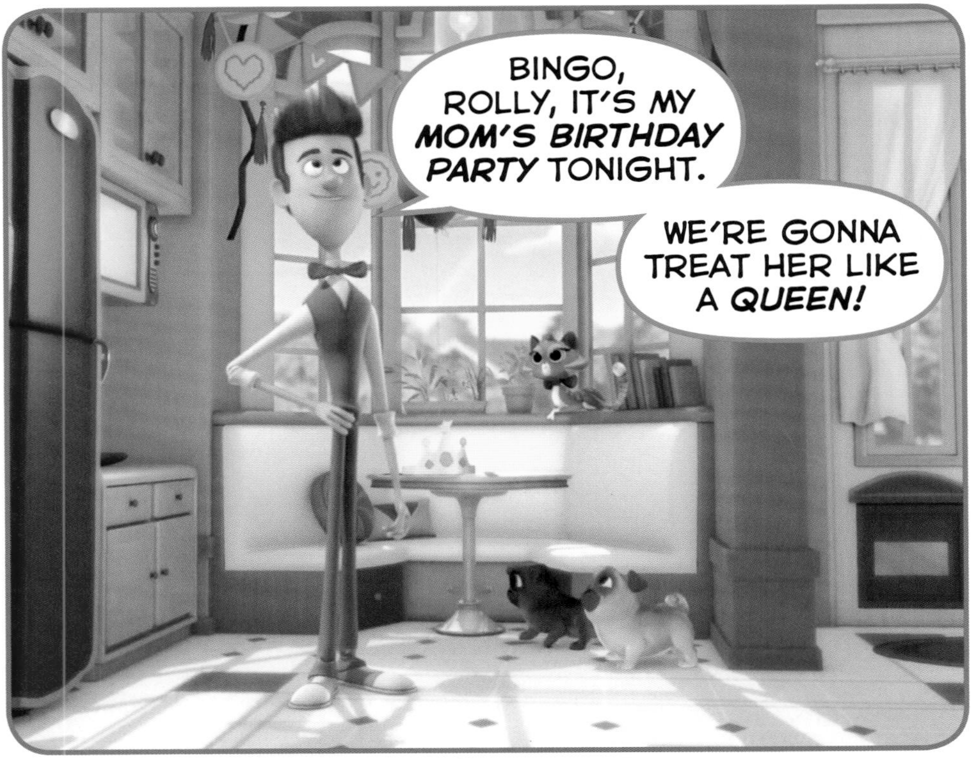
BINGO, ROLLY, IT'S MY *MOM'S BIRTHDAY PARTY* TONIGHT.
WE'RE GONNA TREAT HER LIKE A *QUEEN!*

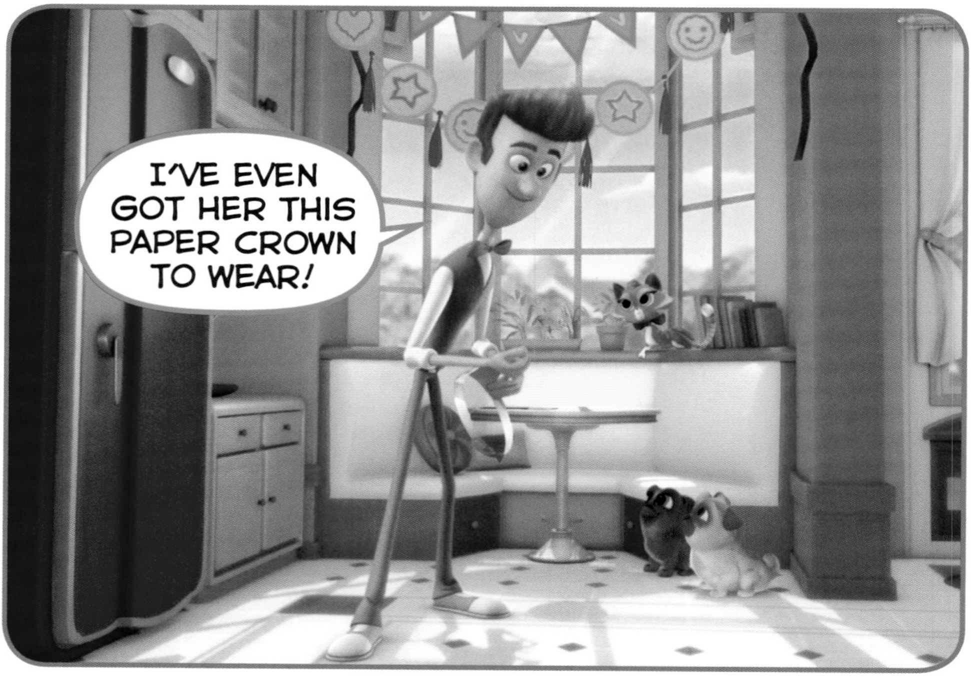
I'VE EVEN GOT HER THIS PAPER CROWN TO WEAR!

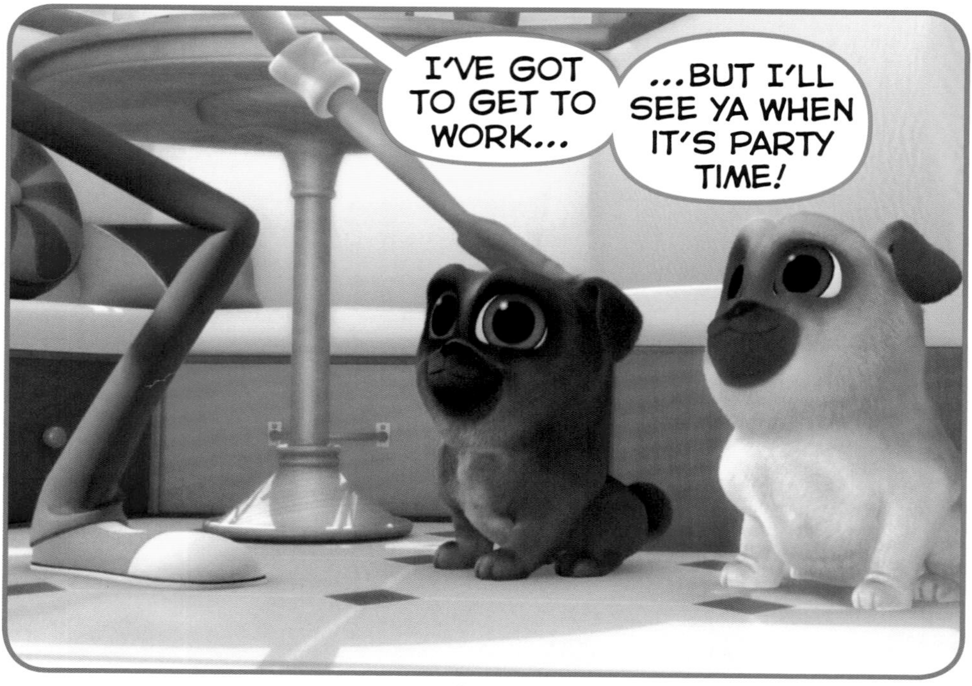
I'VE GOT TO GET TO WORK...
...BUT I'LL SEE YA WHEN IT'S PARTY TIME!

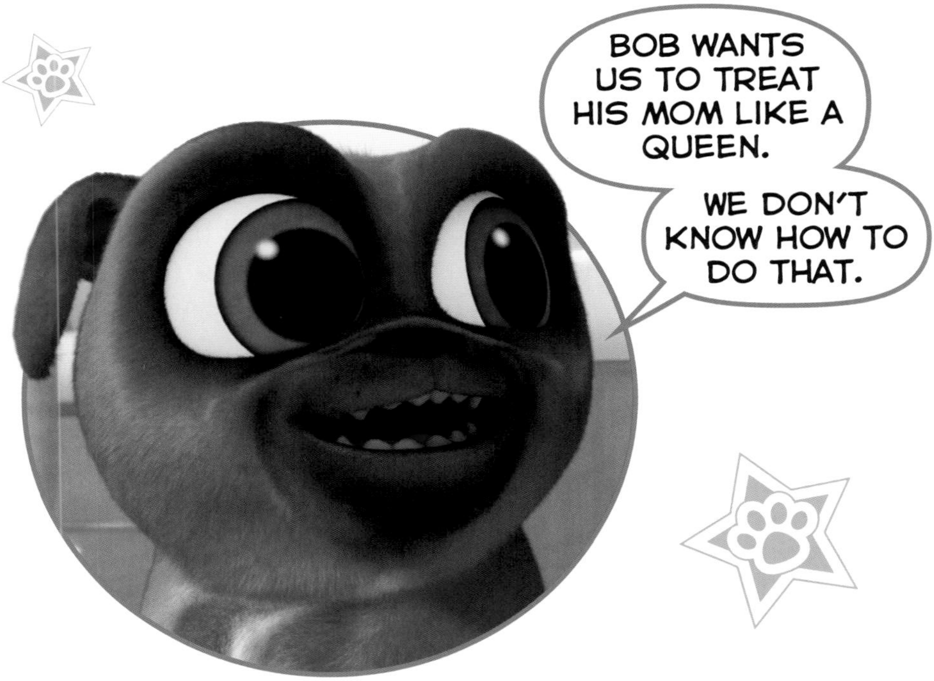
BOB WANTS US TO TREAT HIS MOM LIKE A QUEEN.
WE DON'T KNOW HOW TO DO THAT.

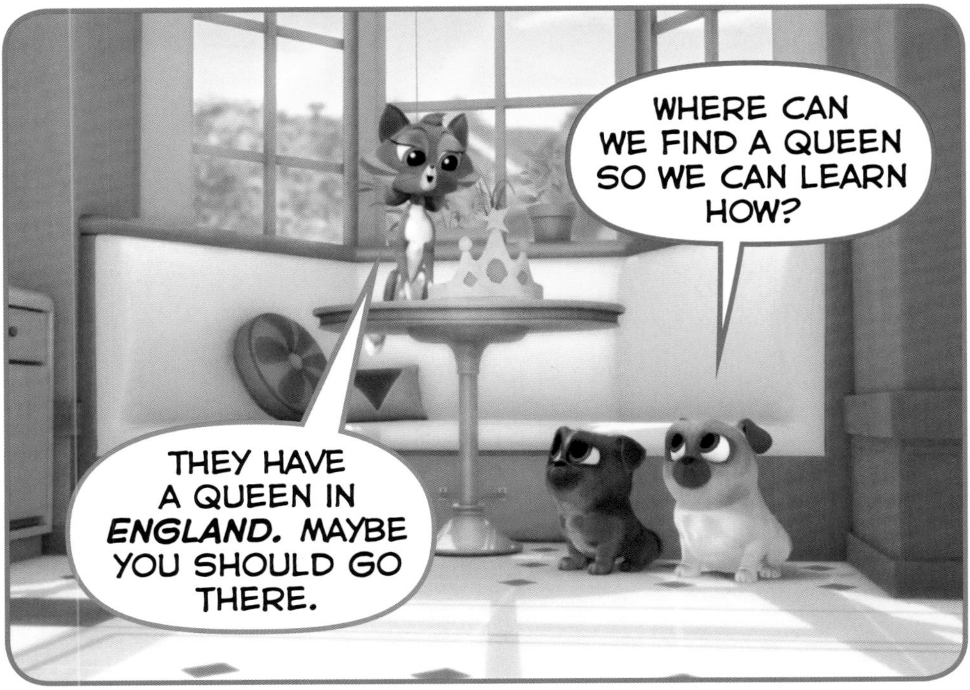
WHERE CAN WE FIND A QUEEN SO WE CAN LEARN HOW?
THEY HAVE A QUEEN IN *ENGLAND.* MAYBE YOU SHOULD GO THERE.

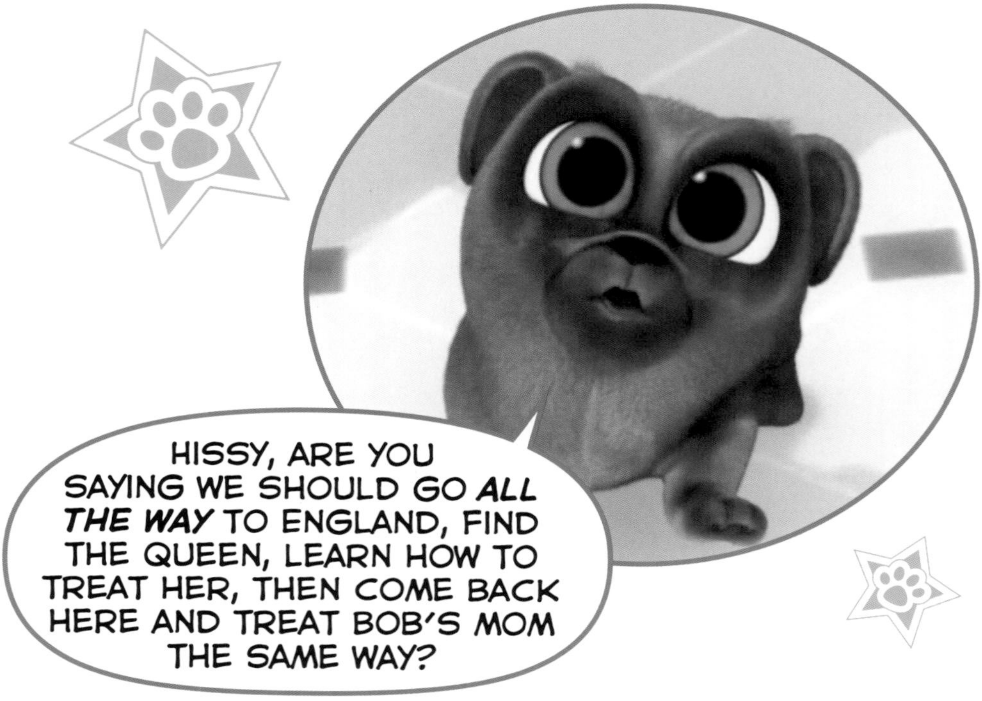
HISSY, ARE YOU SAYING WE SHOULD GO ALL THE WAY TO ENGLAND, FIND THE QUEEN, LEARN HOW TO TREAT HER, THEN COME BACK HERE AND TREAT BOB'S MOM THE SAME WAY?

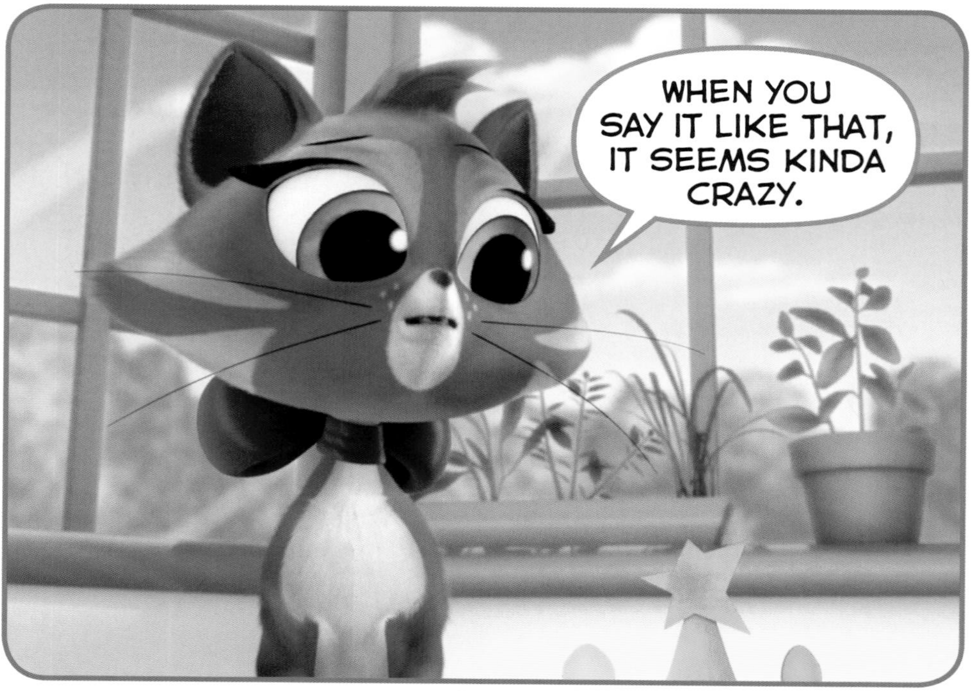
WHEN YOU SAY IT LIKE THAT, IT SEEMS KINDA CRAZY.

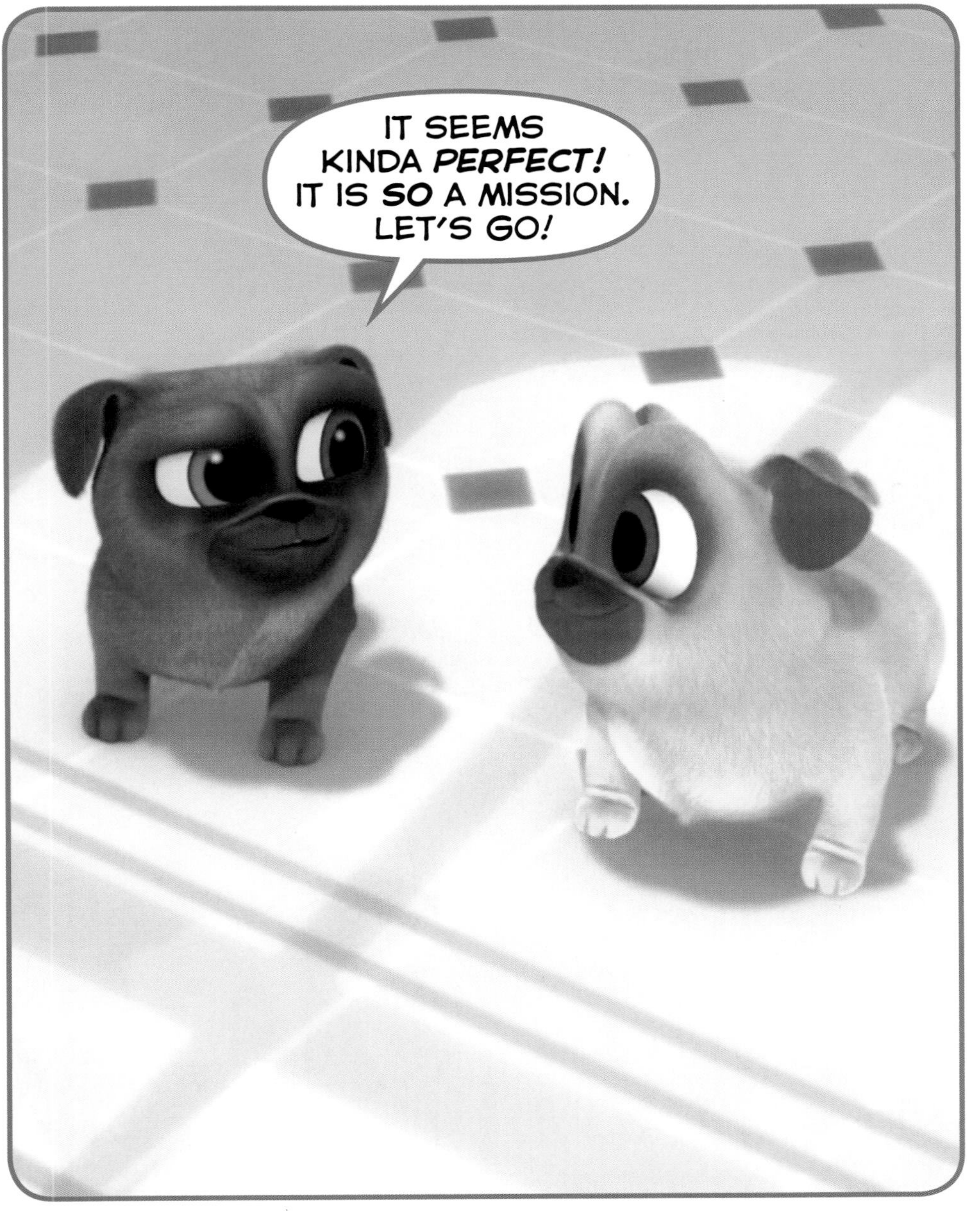
IT SEEMS KINDA *PERFECT!* IT IS **SO** A MISSION. LET'S GO!

BINGO AND ROLLY FLY ACROSS THE OCEAN TO ENGLAND.

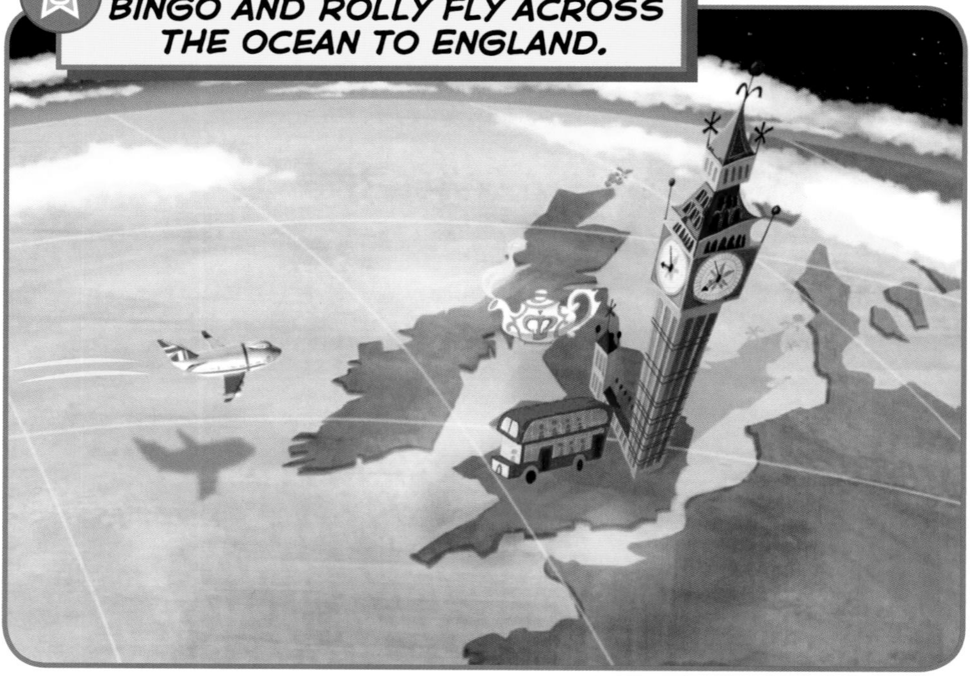

THE QUEEN'S PALACE, ENGLAND.

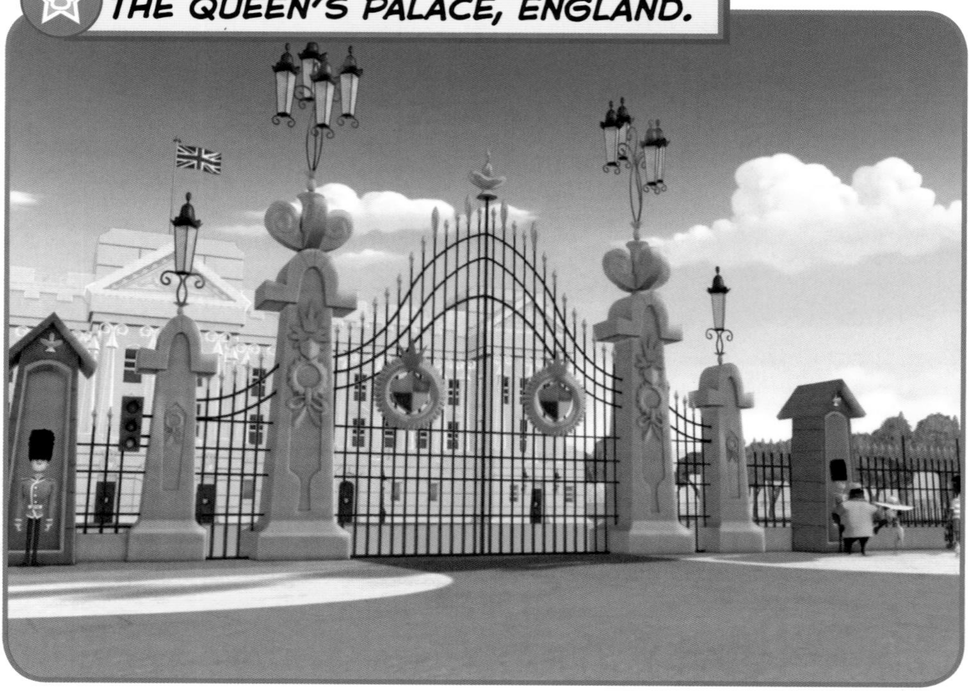

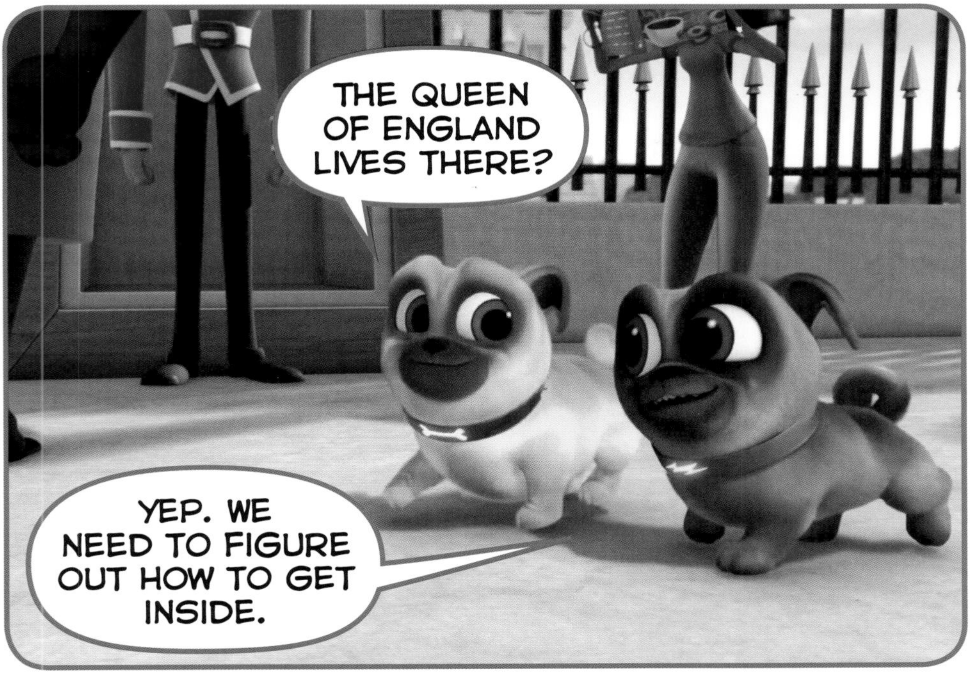
THE QUEEN OF ENGLAND LIVES THERE?
YEP. WE NEED TO FIGURE OUT HOW TO GET INSIDE.

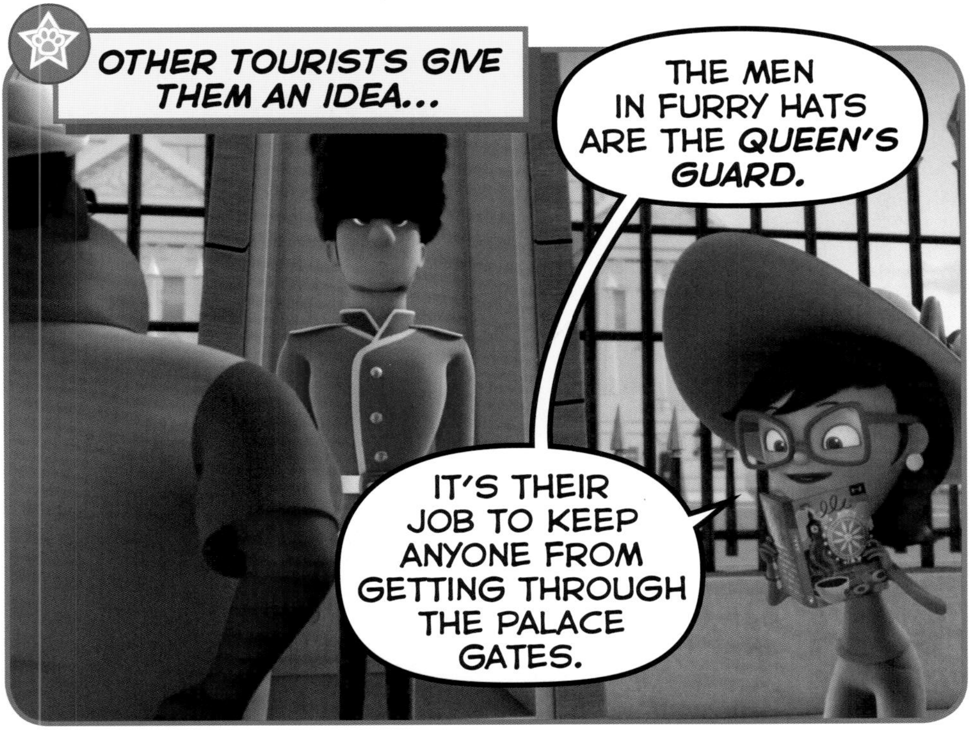
OTHER TOURISTS GIVE THEM AN IDEA...
THE MEN IN FURRY HATS ARE THE *QUEEN'S GUARD.*
IT'S THEIR JOB TO KEEP ANYONE FROM GETTING THROUGH THE PALACE GATES.

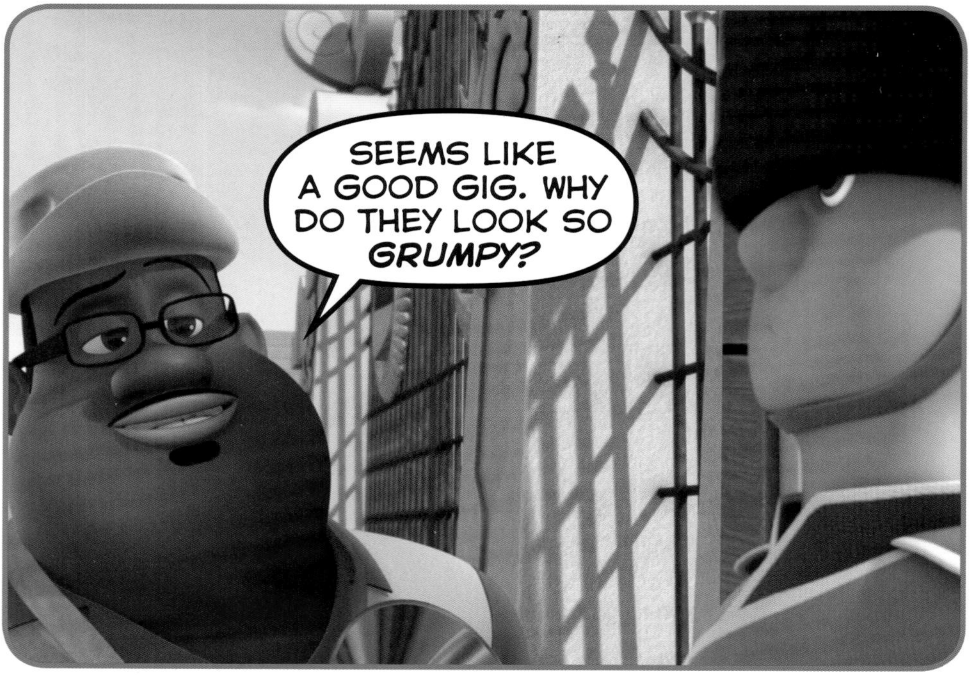
SEEMS LIKE A GOOD GIG. WHY DO THEY LOOK SO *GRUMPY?*

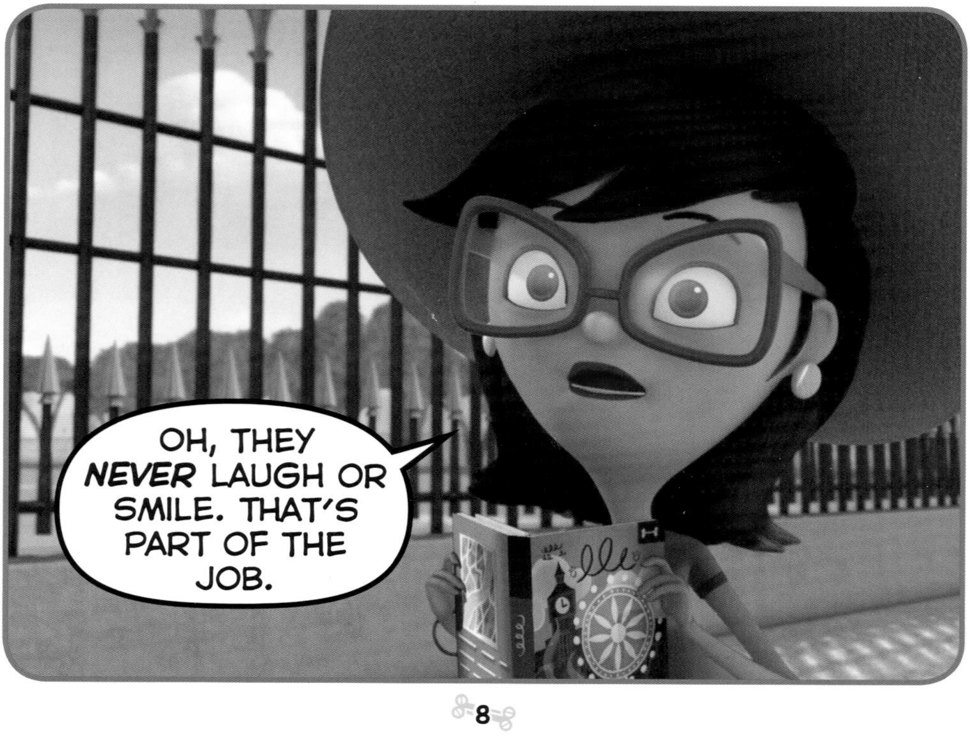
OH, THEY ***NEVER*** LAUGH OR SMILE. THAT'S PART OF THE JOB.

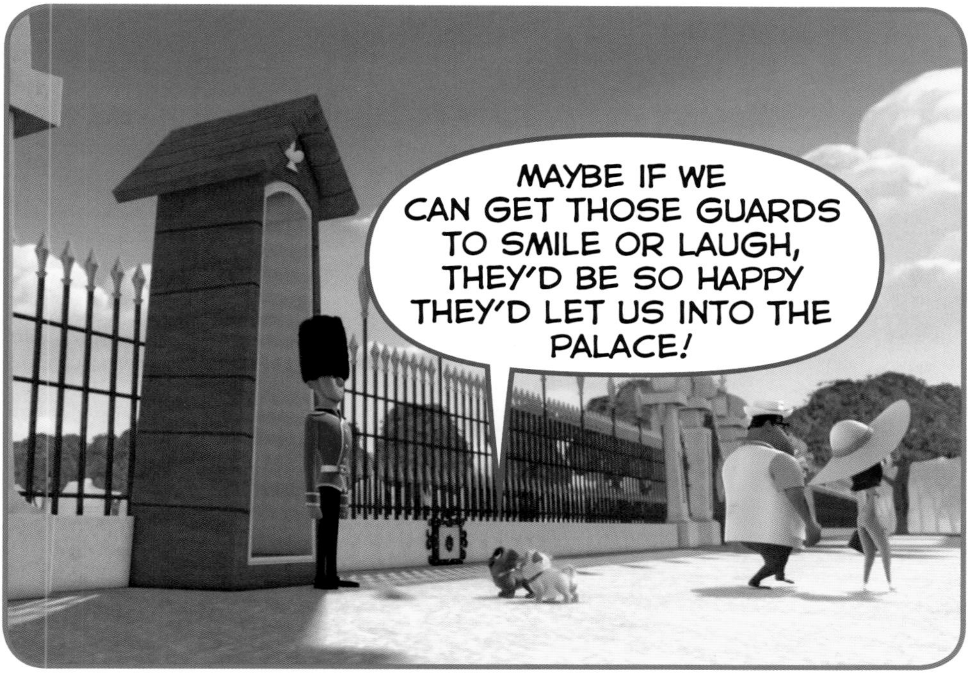
MAYBE IF WE CAN GET THOSE GUARDS TO SMILE OR LAUGH, THEY'D BE SO HAPPY THEY'D LET US INTO THE PALACE!

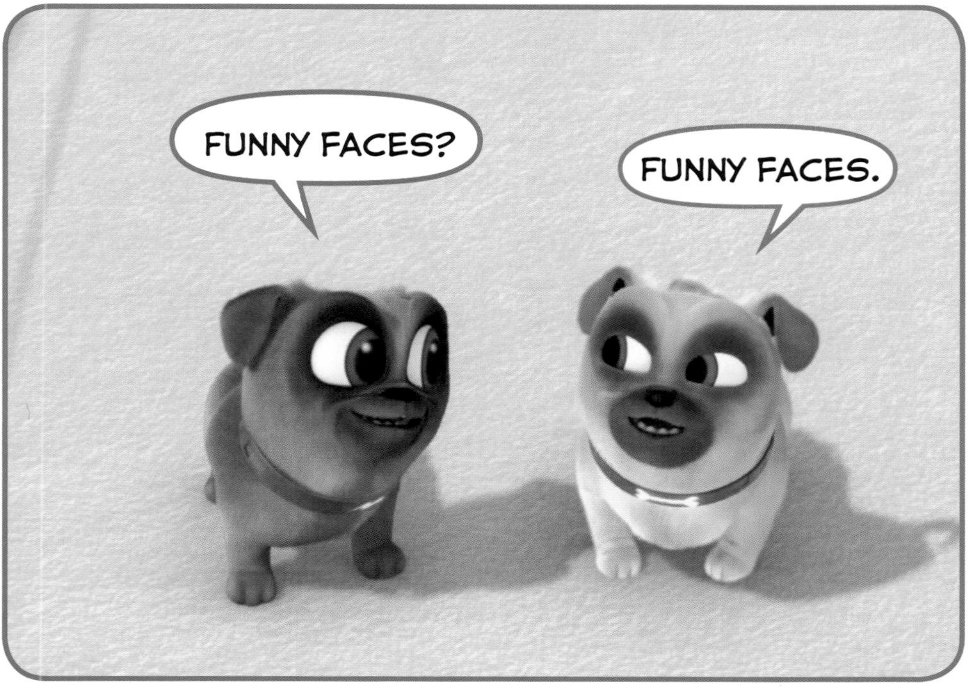
FUNNY FACES?
FUNNY FACES.

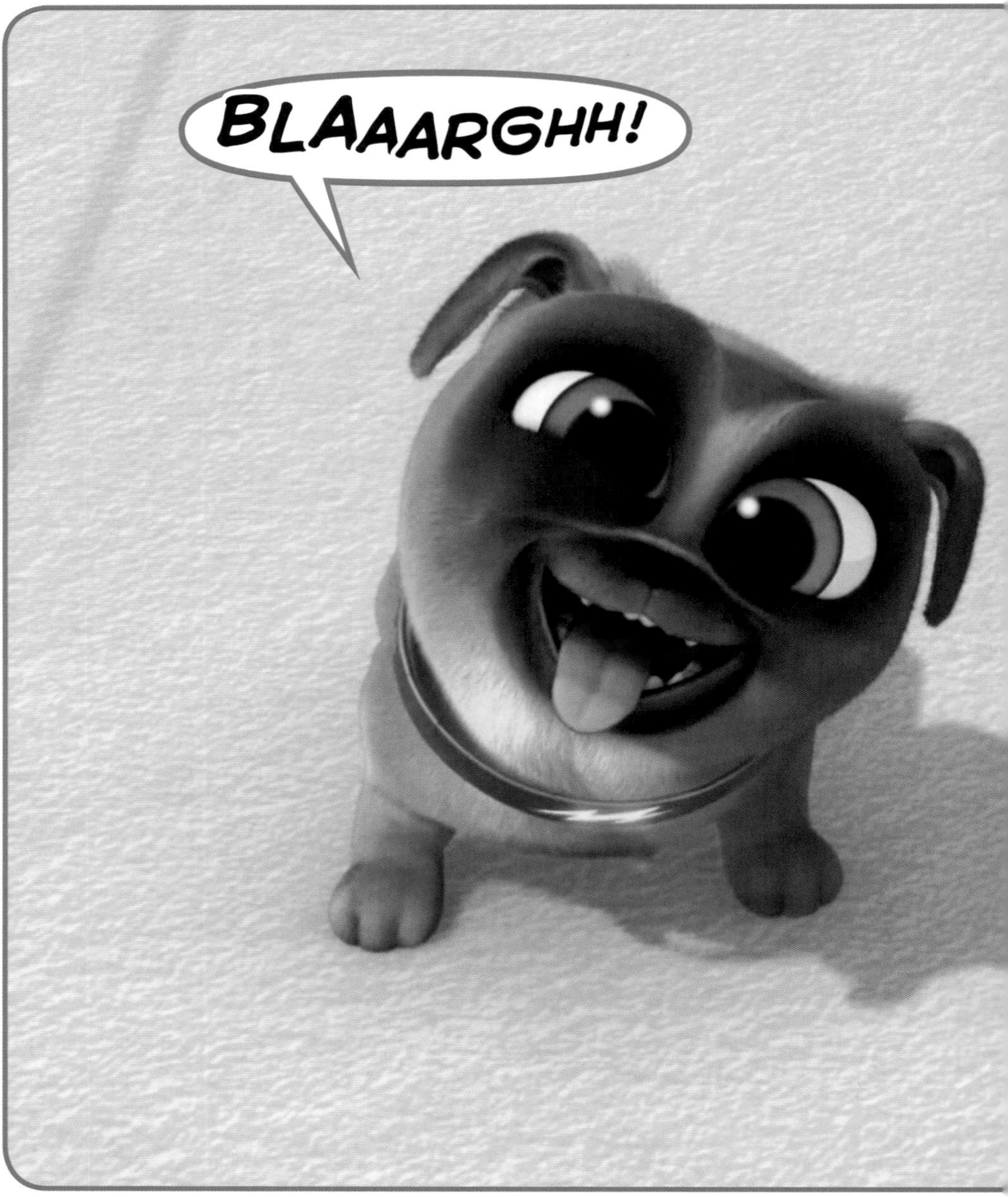
BLAAARGHH!

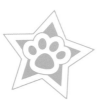

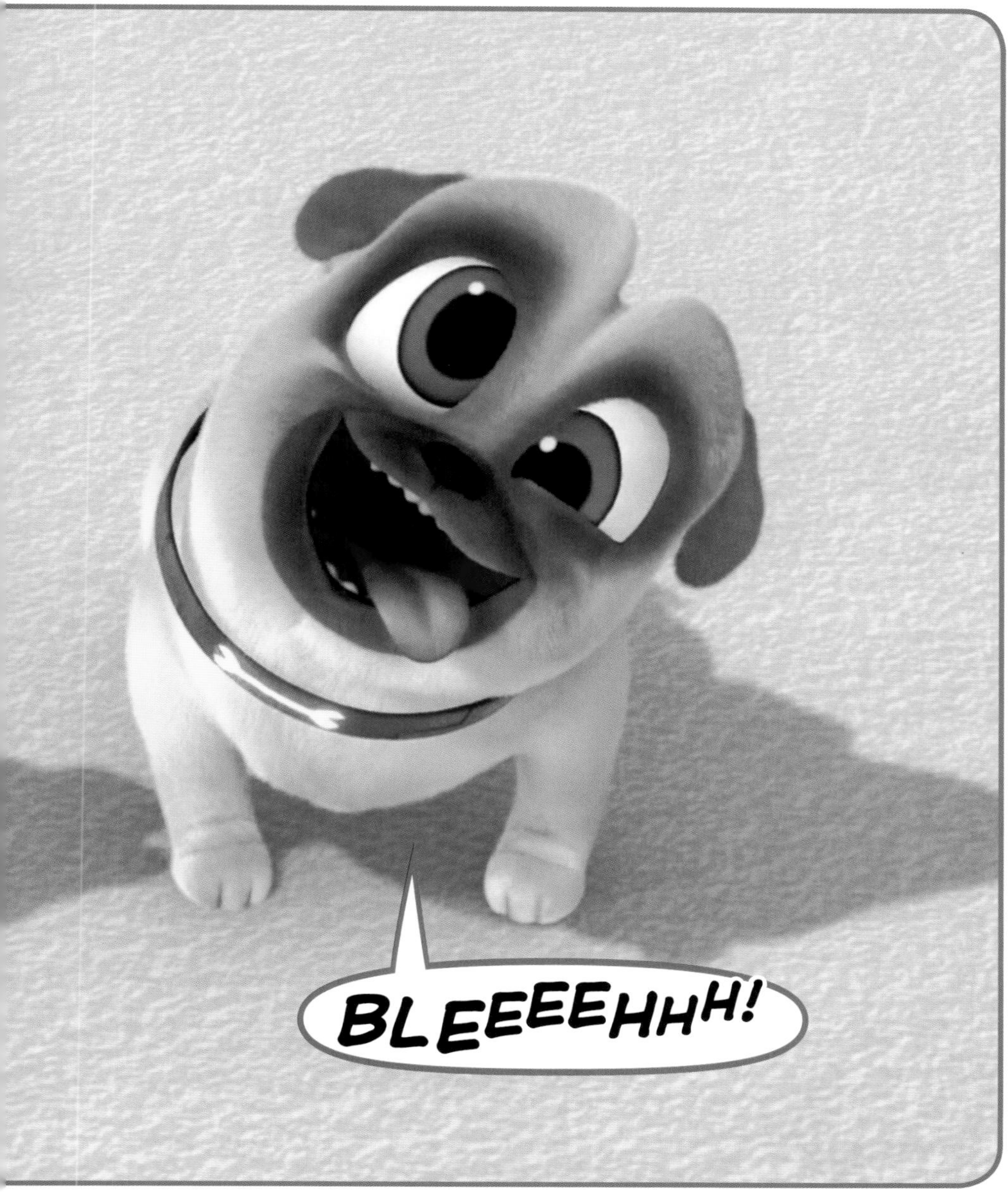
BLEEEEEHHH!

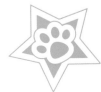

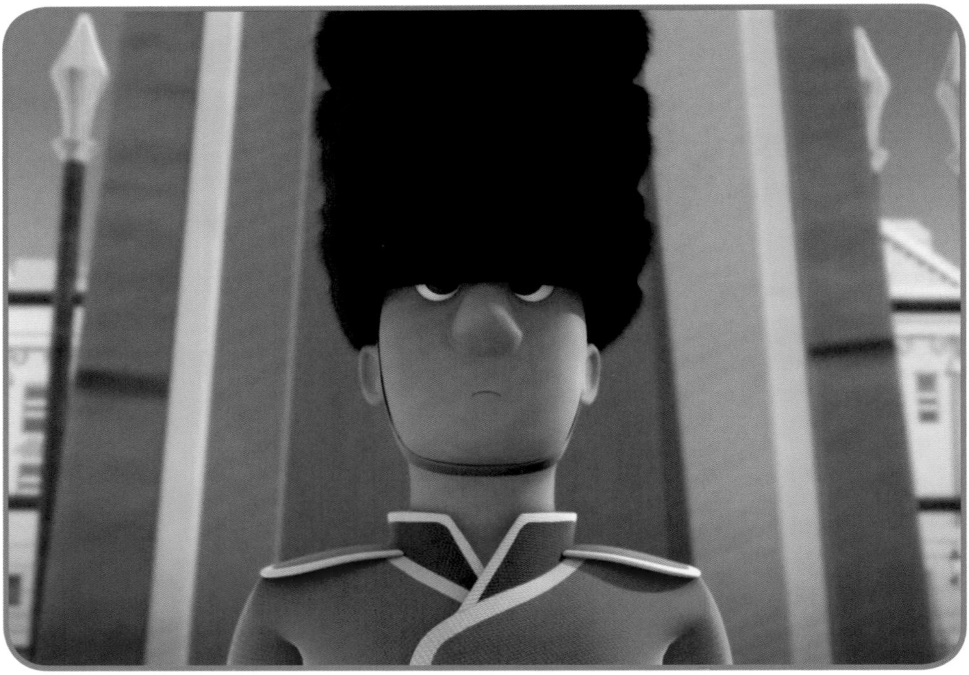

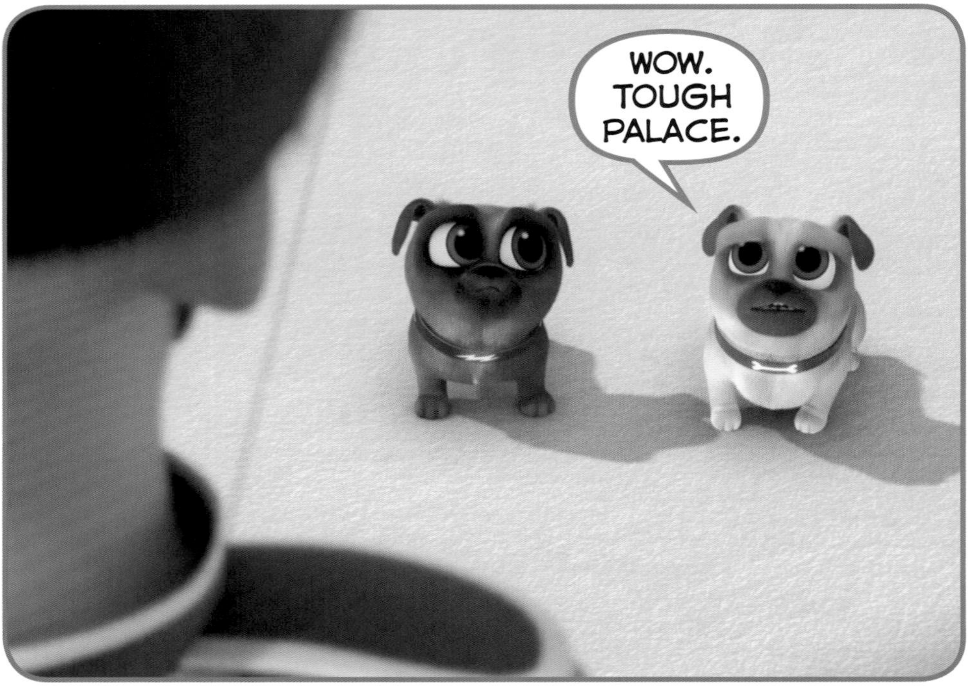
WOW.
TOUGH
PALACE.

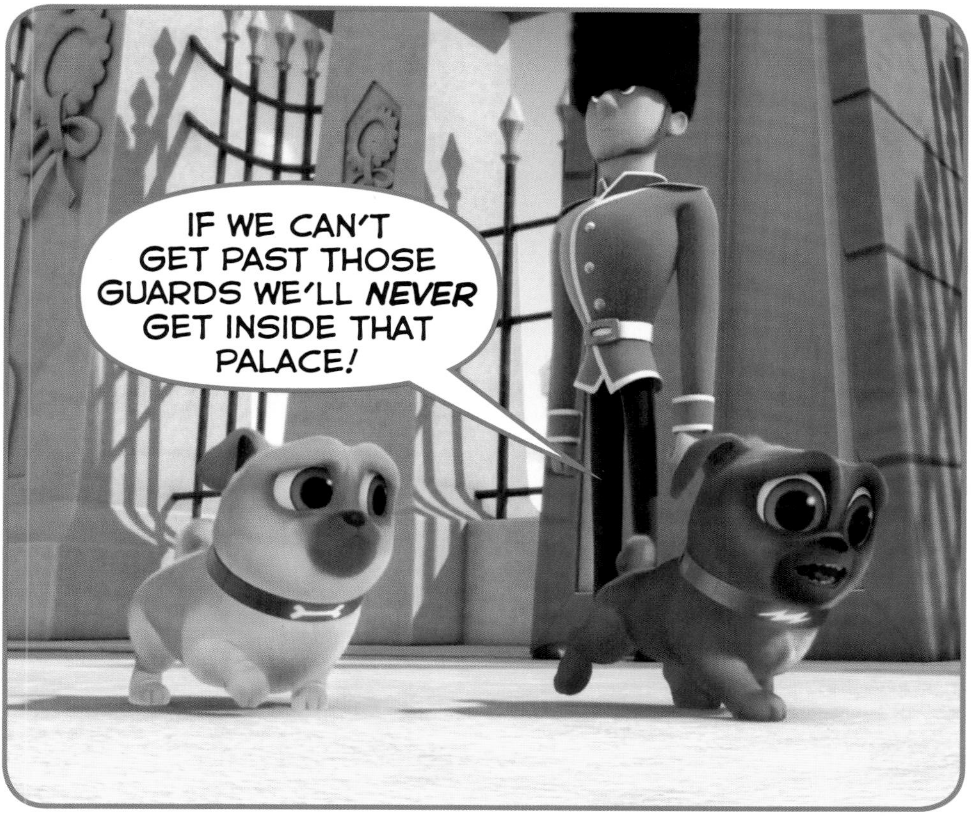
IF WE CAN'T GET PAST THOSE GUARDS WE'LL ***NEVER*** GET INSIDE THAT PALACE!

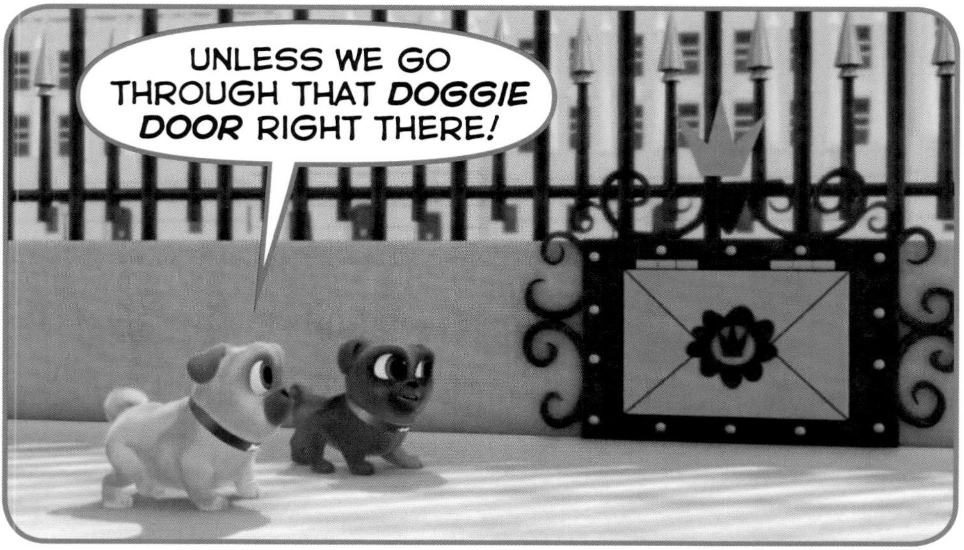
UNLESS WE GO THROUGH THAT ***DOGGIE DOOR*** RIGHT THERE!

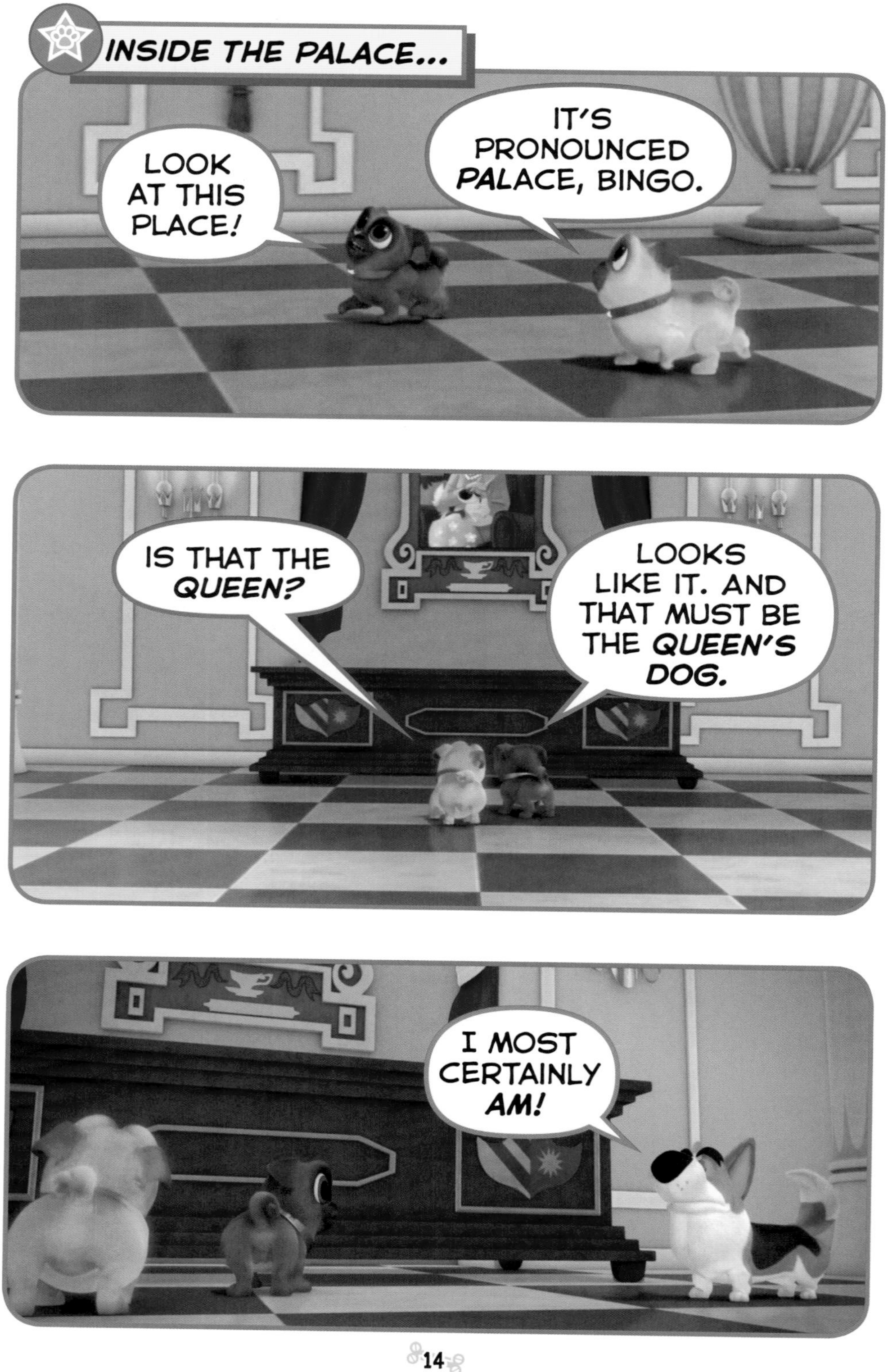
INSIDE THE PALACE...
LOOK AT THIS PLACE!
IT'S PRONOUNCED PALACE, BINGO.
IS THAT THE QUEEN?
LOOKS LIKE IT. AND THAT MUST BE THE QUEEN'S DOG.
I MOST CERTAINLY AM!

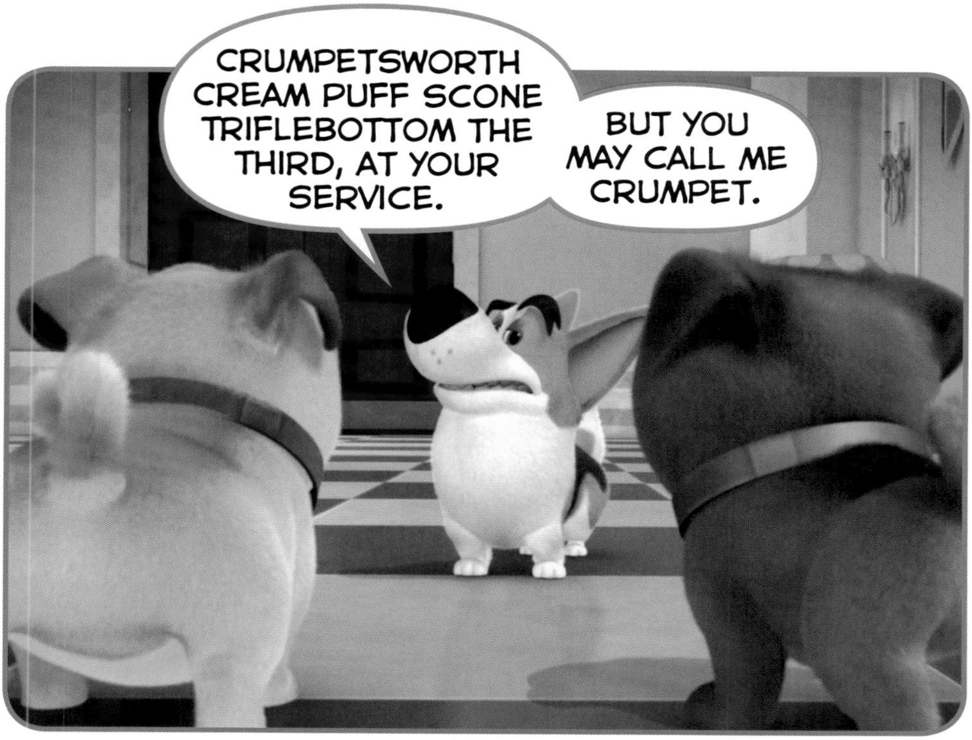
CRUMPETSWORTH CREAM PUFF SCONE TRIFLEBOTTOM THE THIRD, AT YOUR SERVICE.
BUT YOU MAY CALL ME CRUMPET.

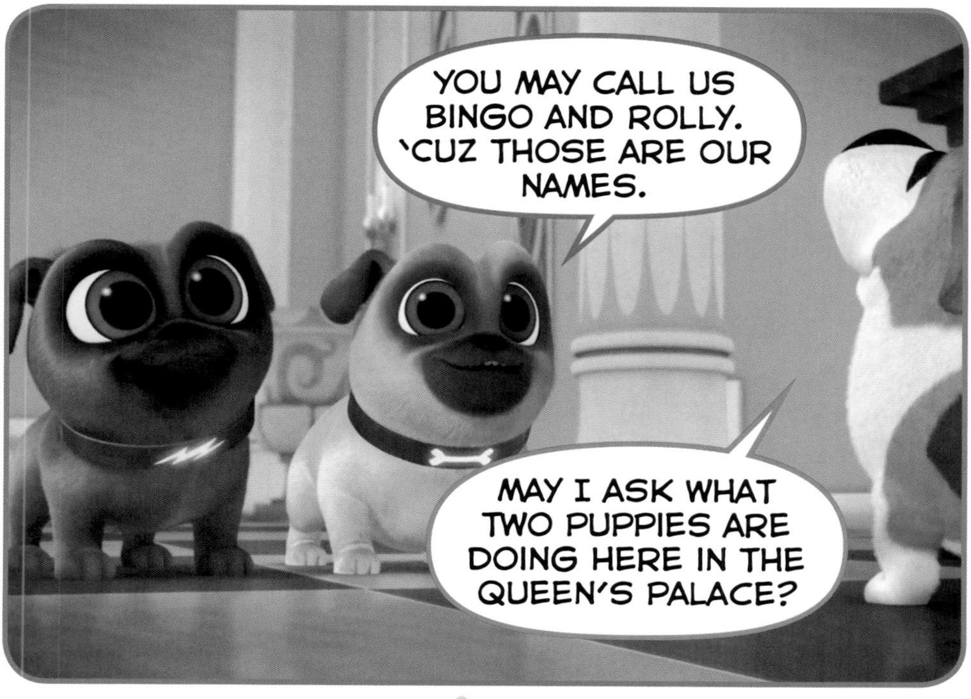
YOU MAY CALL US BINGO AND ROLLY. 'CUZ THOSE ARE OUR NAMES.
MAY I ASK WHAT TWO PUPPIES ARE DOING HERE IN THE QUEEN'S PALACE?

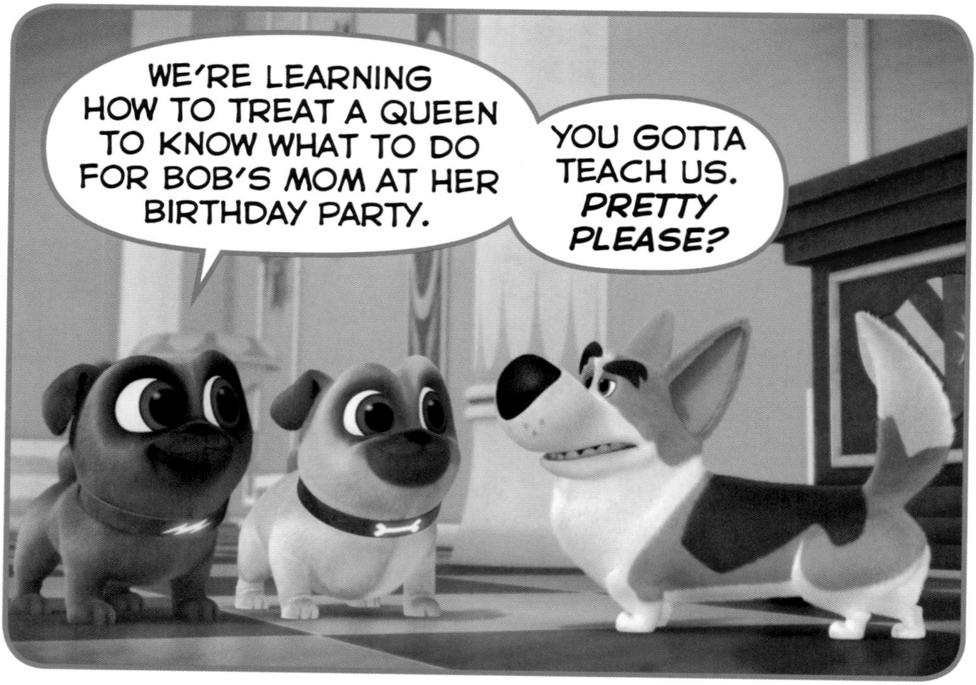
WE'RE LEARNING HOW TO TREAT A QUEEN TO KNOW WHAT TO DO FOR BOB'S MOM AT HER BIRTHDAY PARTY.
YOU GOTTA TEACH US. *PRETTY PLEASE?*

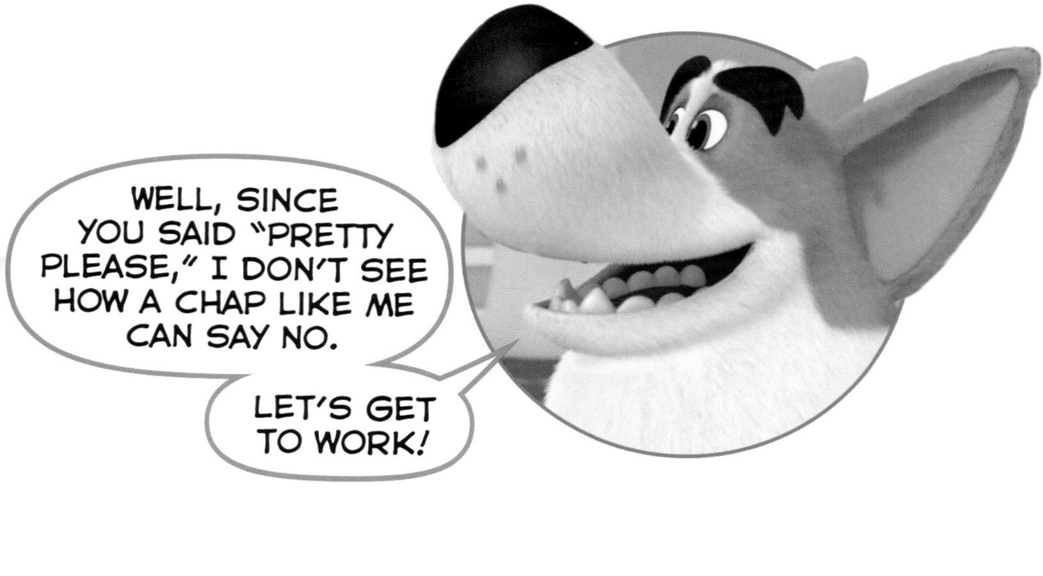
WELL, SINCE YOU SAID "PRETTY PLEASE," I DON'T SEE HOW A CHAP LIKE ME CAN SAY NO.
LET'S GET TO WORK!

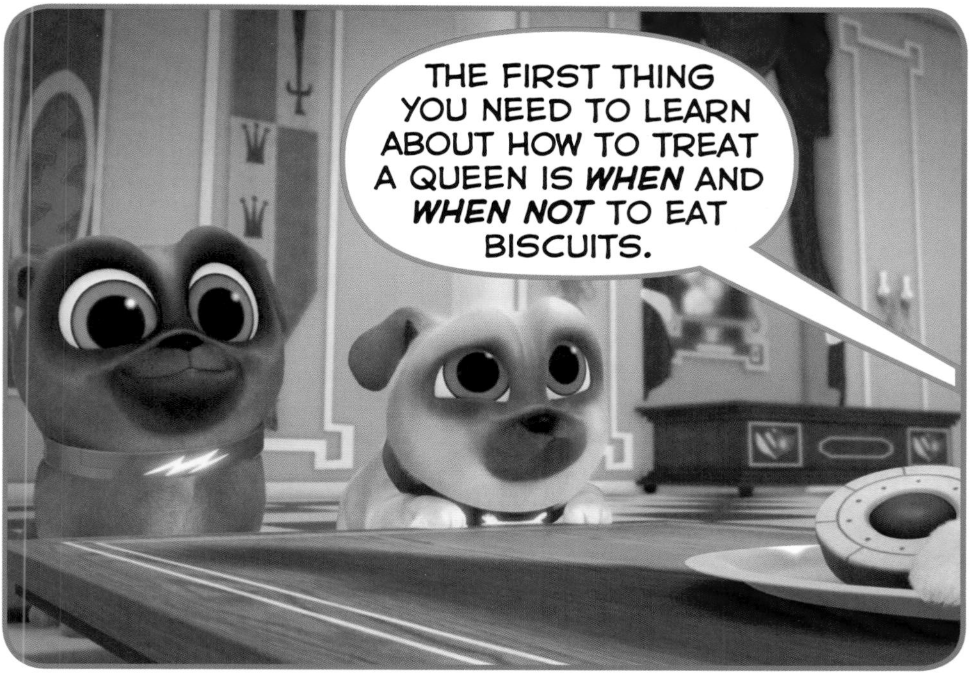
THE FIRST THING YOU NEED TO LEARN ABOUT HOW TO TREAT A QUEEN IS *WHEN* AND *WHEN NOT* TO EAT BISCUITS.

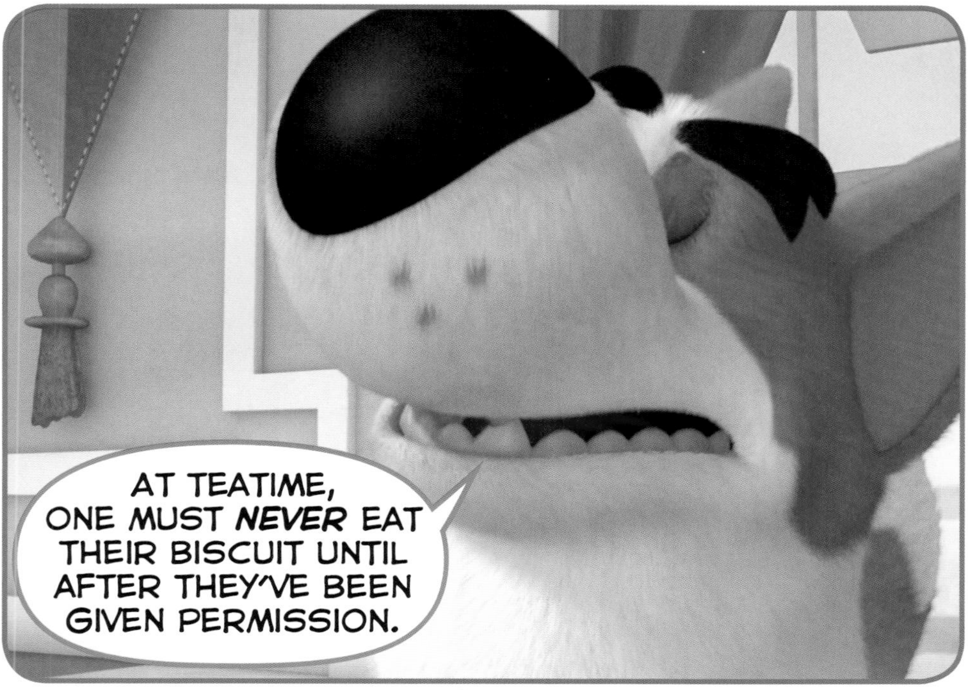
AT TEATIME, ONE MUST *NEVER* EAT THEIR BISCUIT UNTIL AFTER THEY'VE BEEN GIVEN PERMISSION.

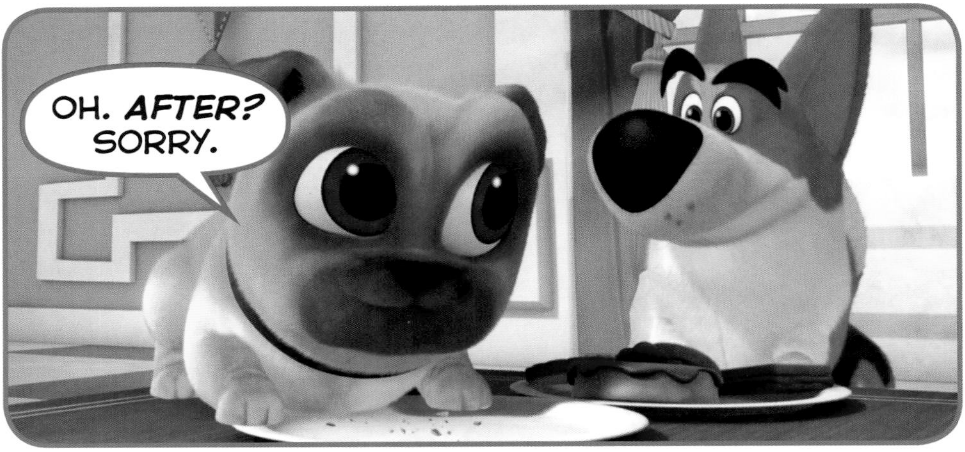
OH. *AFTER?* SORRY.

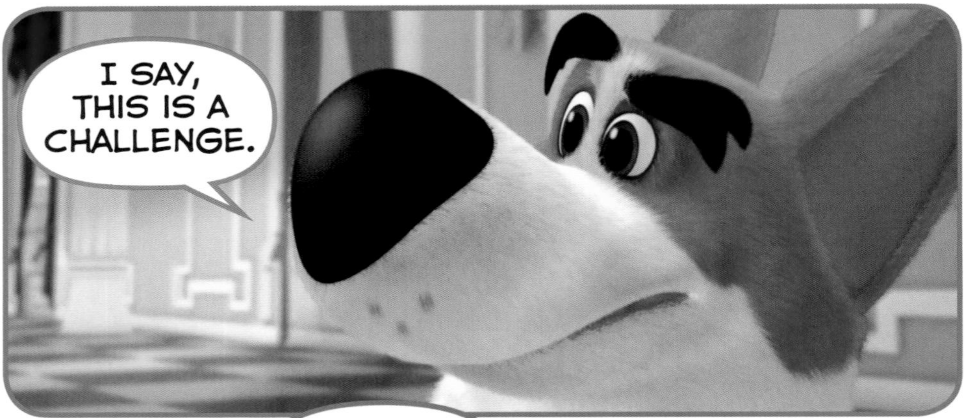
I SAY, THIS IS A CHALLENGE.

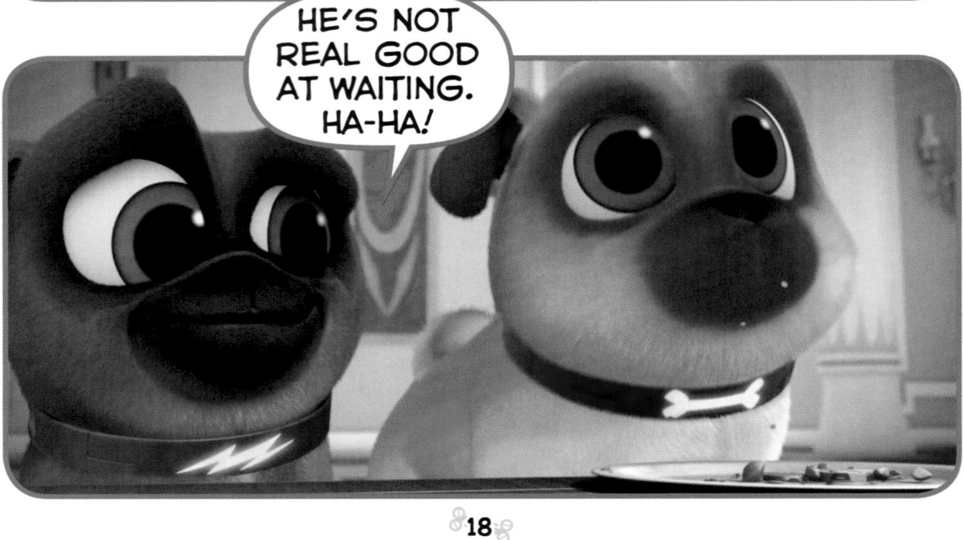
HE'S NOT REAL GOOD AT WAITING. HA-HA!

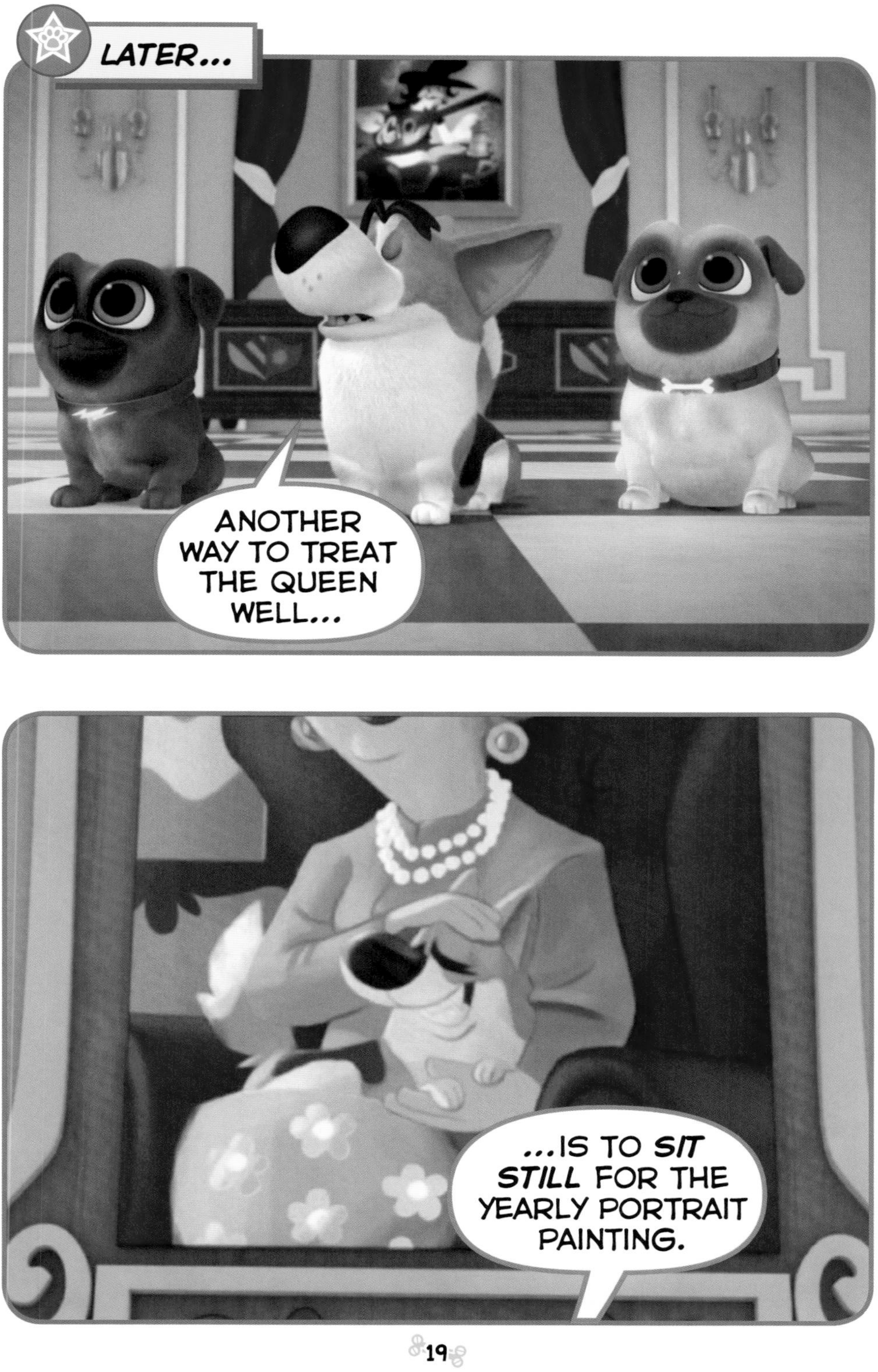

LATER...
ANOTHER WAY TO TREAT THE QUEEN WELL...
...IS TO *SIT STILL* FOR THE YEARLY PORTRAIT PAINTING.

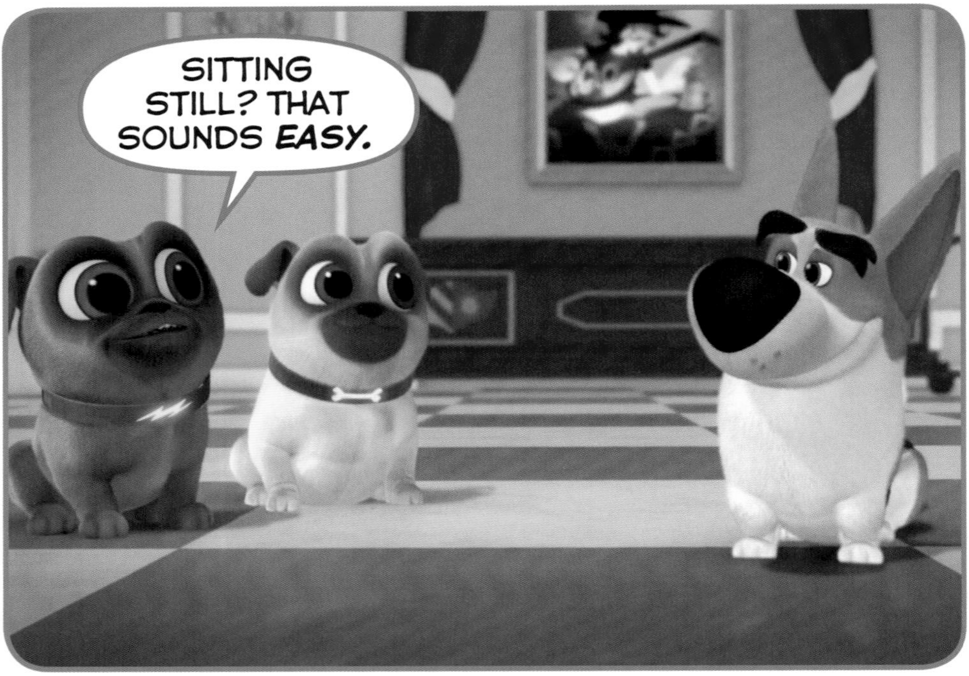
SITTING STILL? THAT SOUNDS *EASY.*

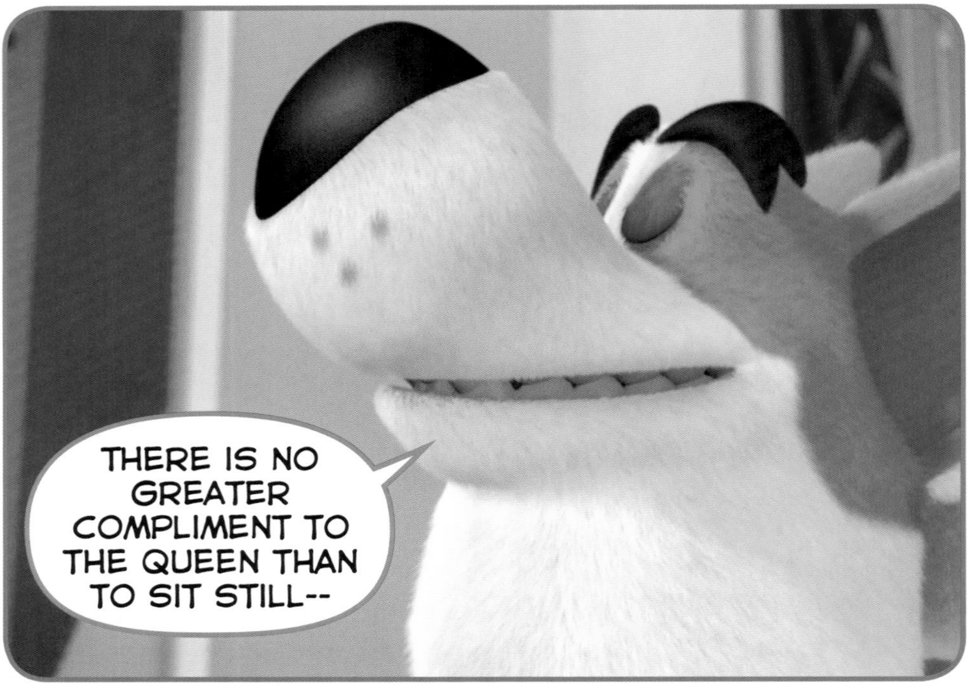
THERE IS NO GREATER COMPLIMENT TO THE QUEEN THAN TO SIT STILL--

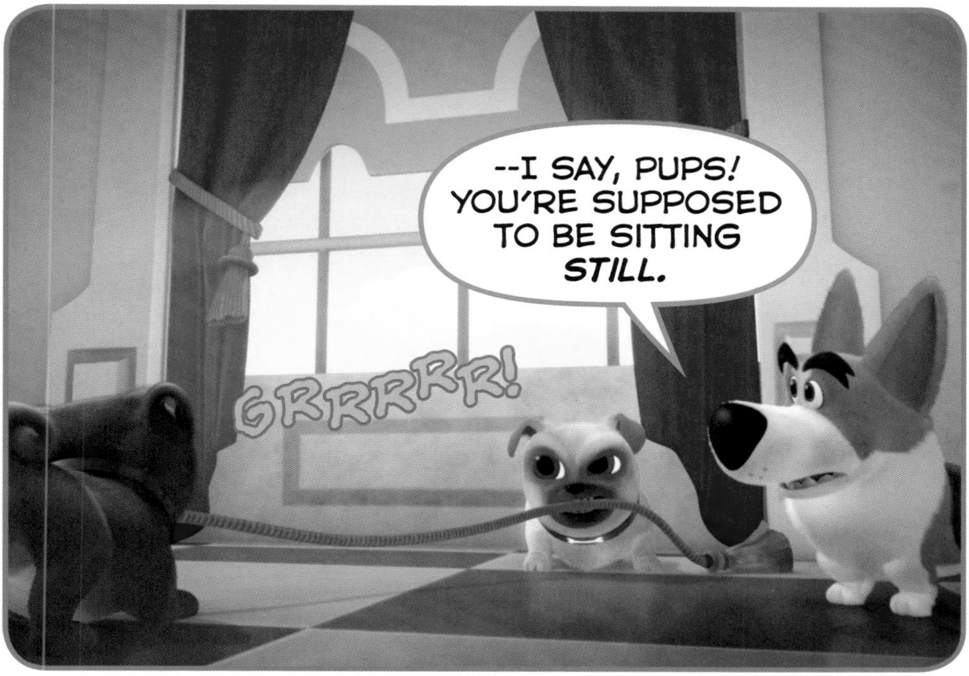
--I SAY, PUPS! YOU'RE SUPPOSED TO BE SITTING STILL.
GRRRRR!

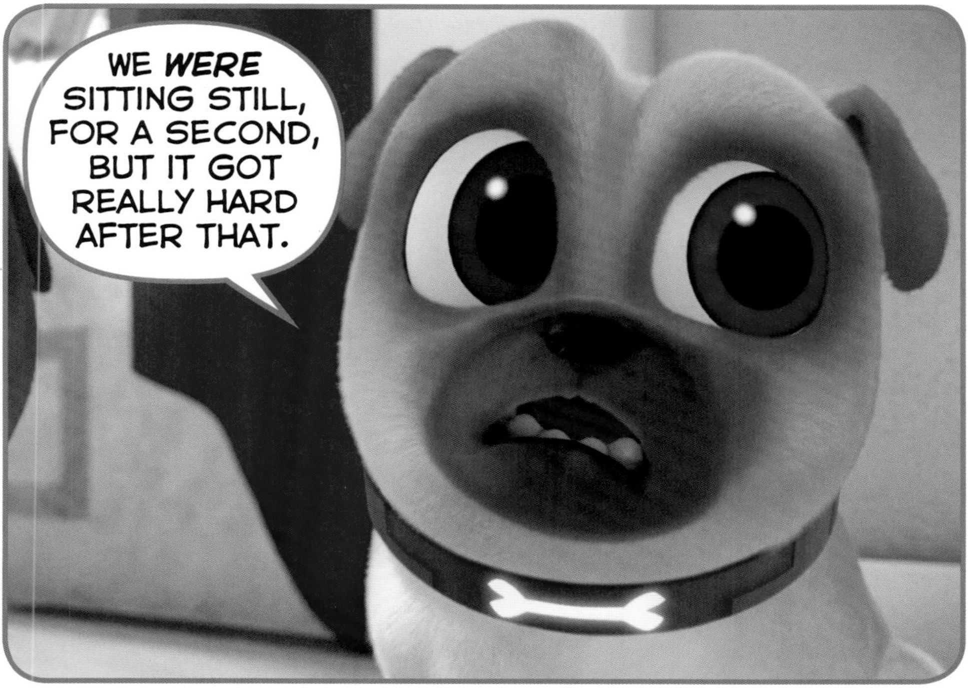
WE WERE SITTING STILL, FOR A SECOND, BUT IT GOT REALLY HARD AFTER THAT.

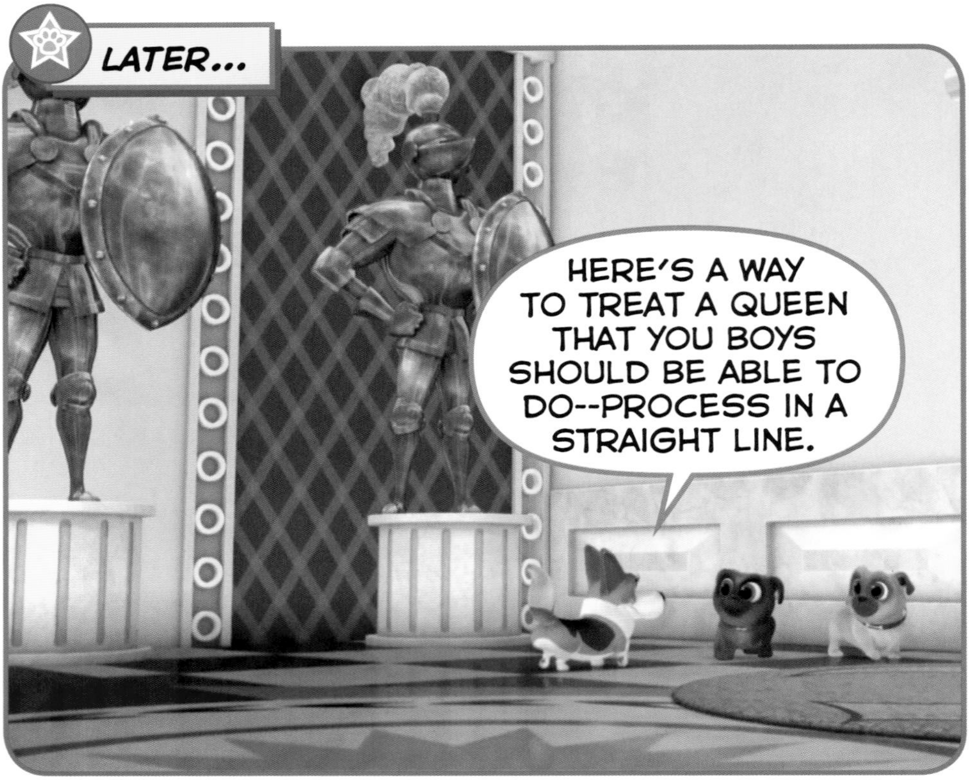
LATER...
HERE'S A WAY TO TREAT A QUEEN THAT YOU BOYS SHOULD BE ABLE TO DO--PROCESS IN A STRAIGHT LINE.

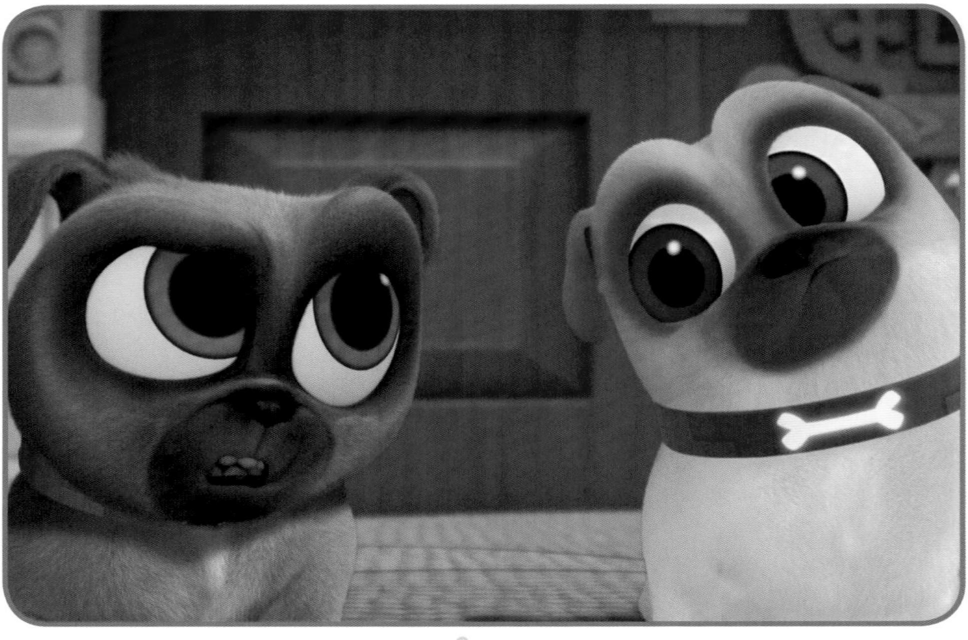

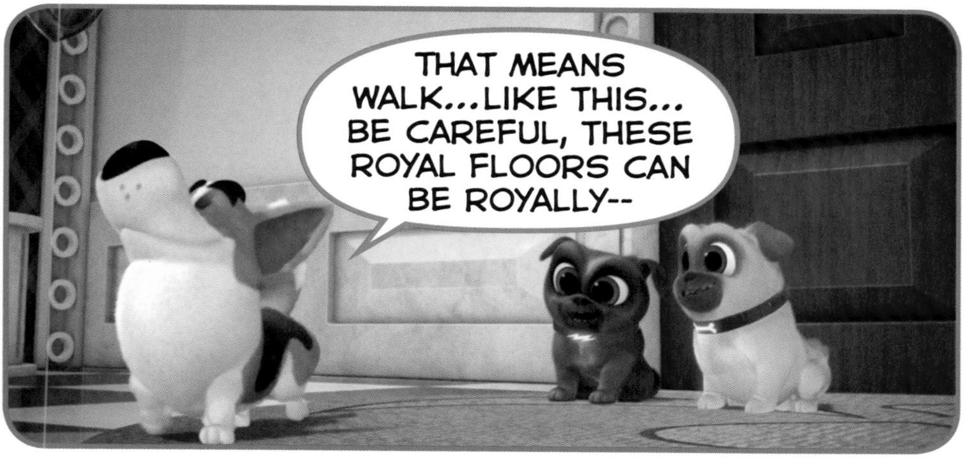
THAT MEANS WALK...LIKE THIS... BE CAREFUL, THESE ROYAL FLOORS CAN BE ROYALLY--

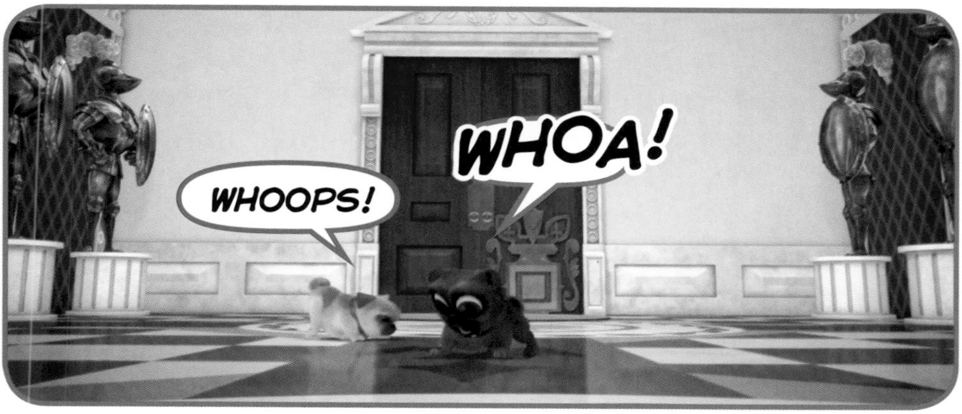
WHOOPS!
WHOA!

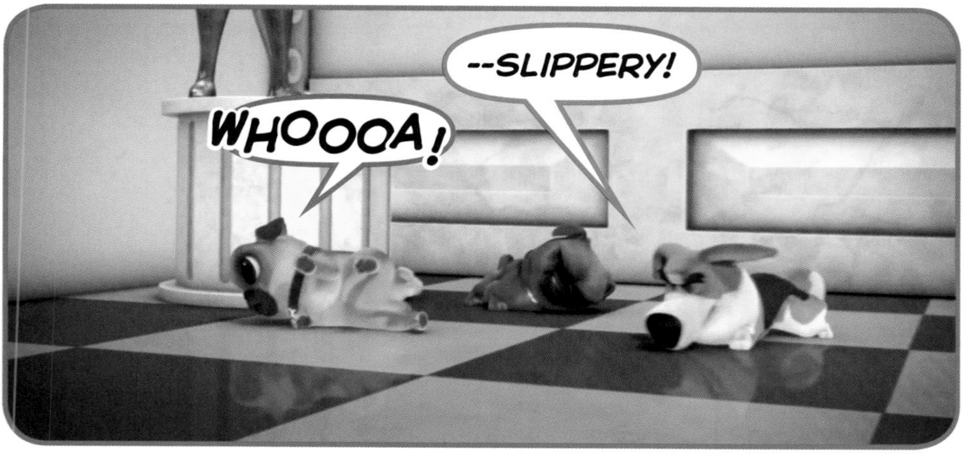
WHOOOA!
--SLIPPERY!

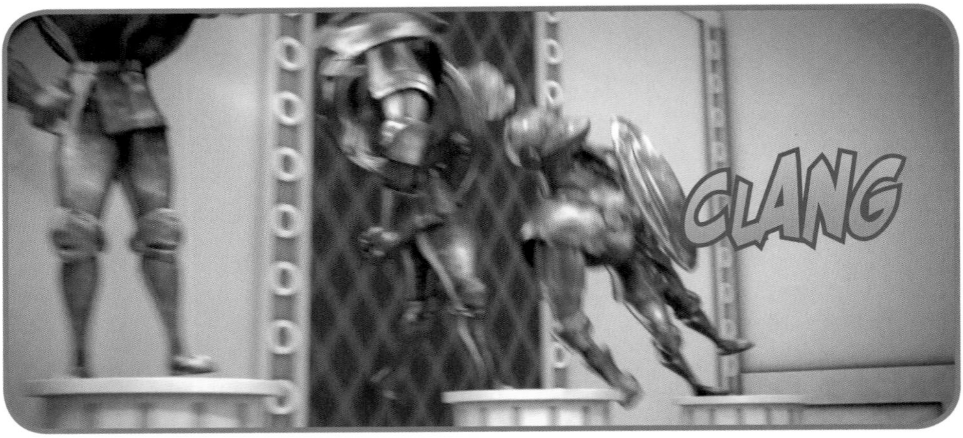
CLANG

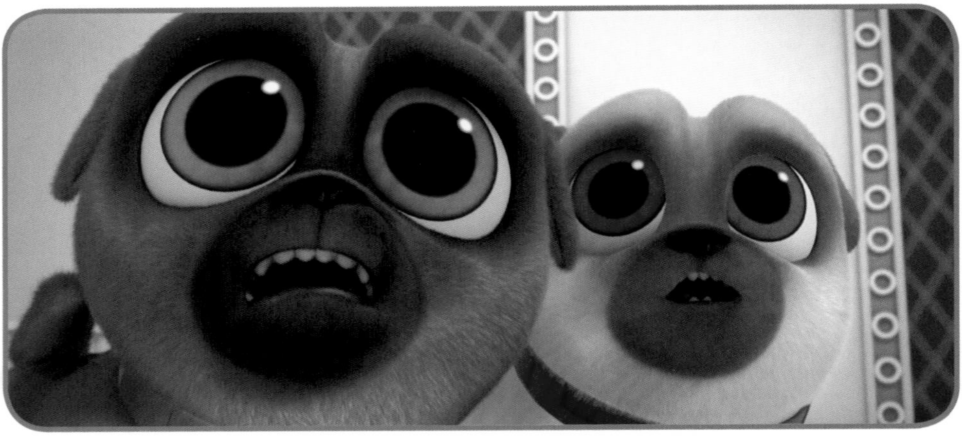

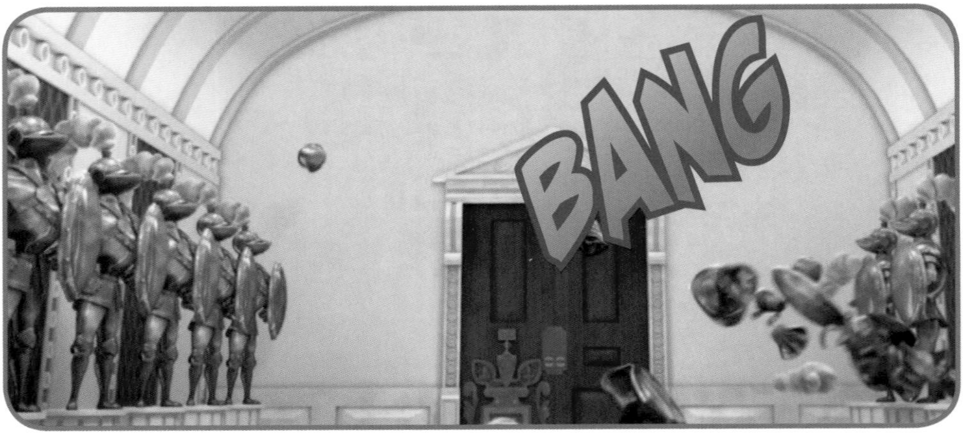
BANG

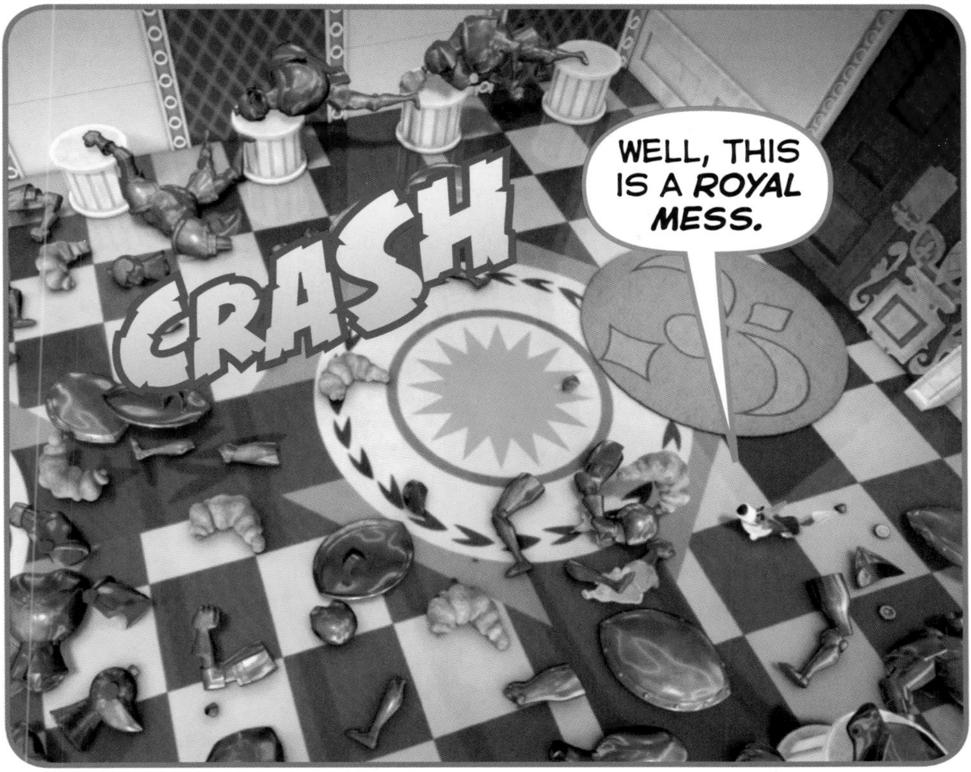
CRASH
WELL, THIS IS A *ROYAL* MESS.

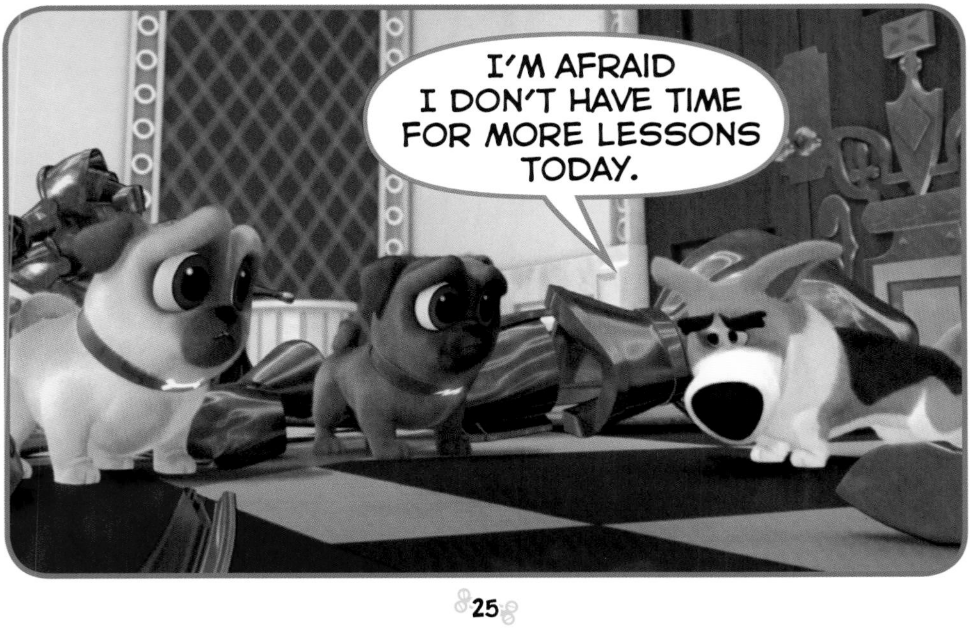
I'M AFRAID I DON'T HAVE TIME FOR MORE LESSONS TODAY.

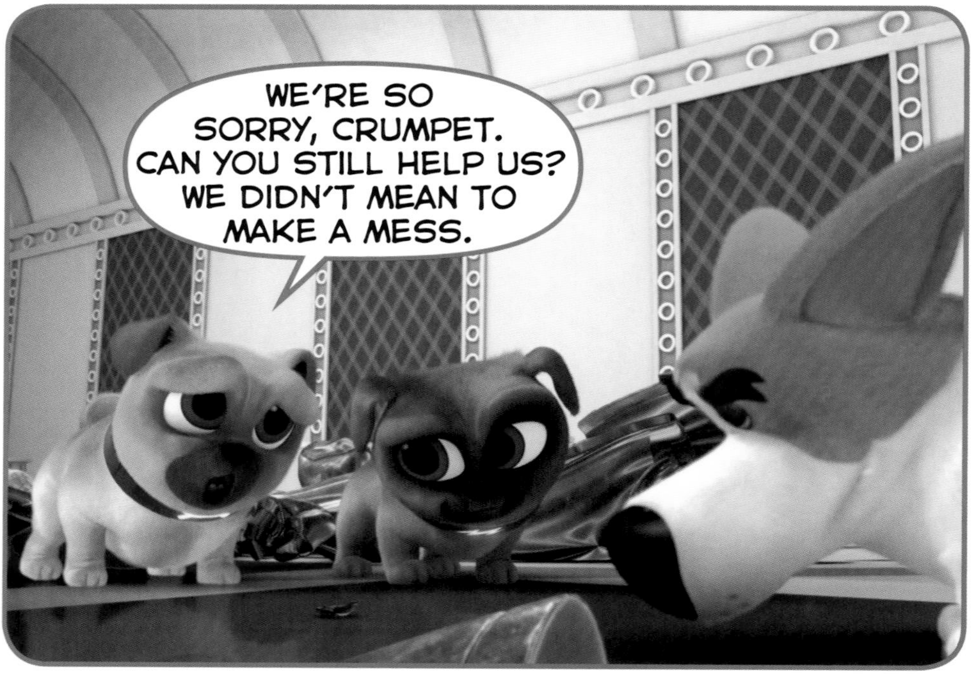
WE'RE SO SORRY, CRUMPET. CAN YOU STILL HELP US? WE DIDN'T MEAN TO MAKE A MESS.

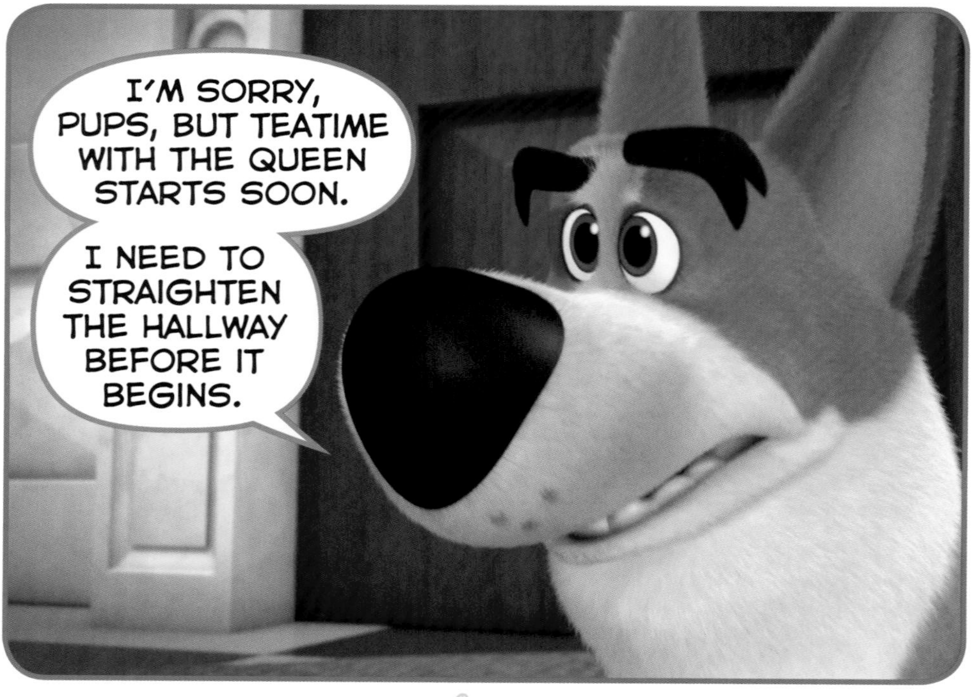
I'M SORRY, PUPS, BUT TEATIME WITH THE QUEEN STARTS SOON.
I NEED TO STRAIGHTEN THE HALLWAY BEFORE IT BEGINS.

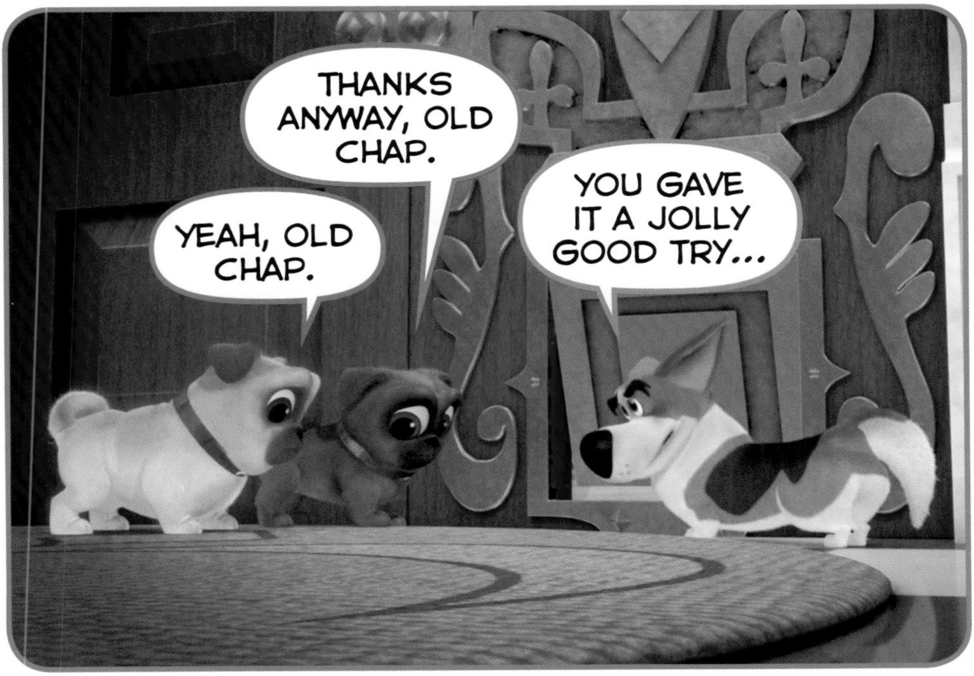
THANKS ANYWAY, OLD CHAP.
YEAH, OLD CHAP.
YOU GAVE IT A JOLLY GOOD TRY...

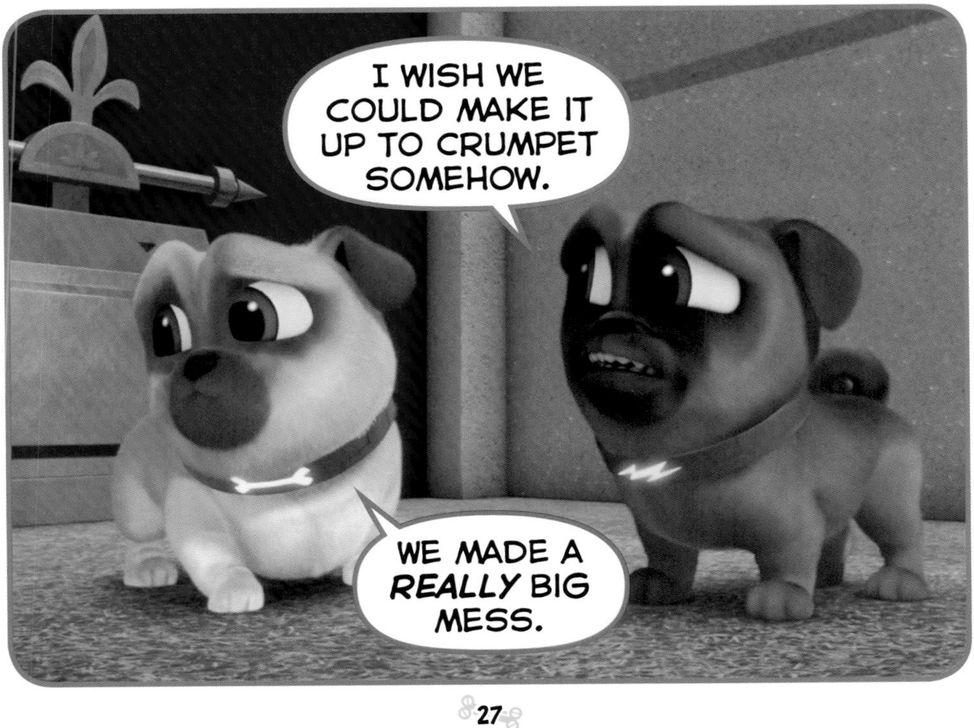
I WISH WE COULD MAKE IT UP TO CRUMPET SOMEHOW.
WE MADE A *REALLY* BIG MESS.

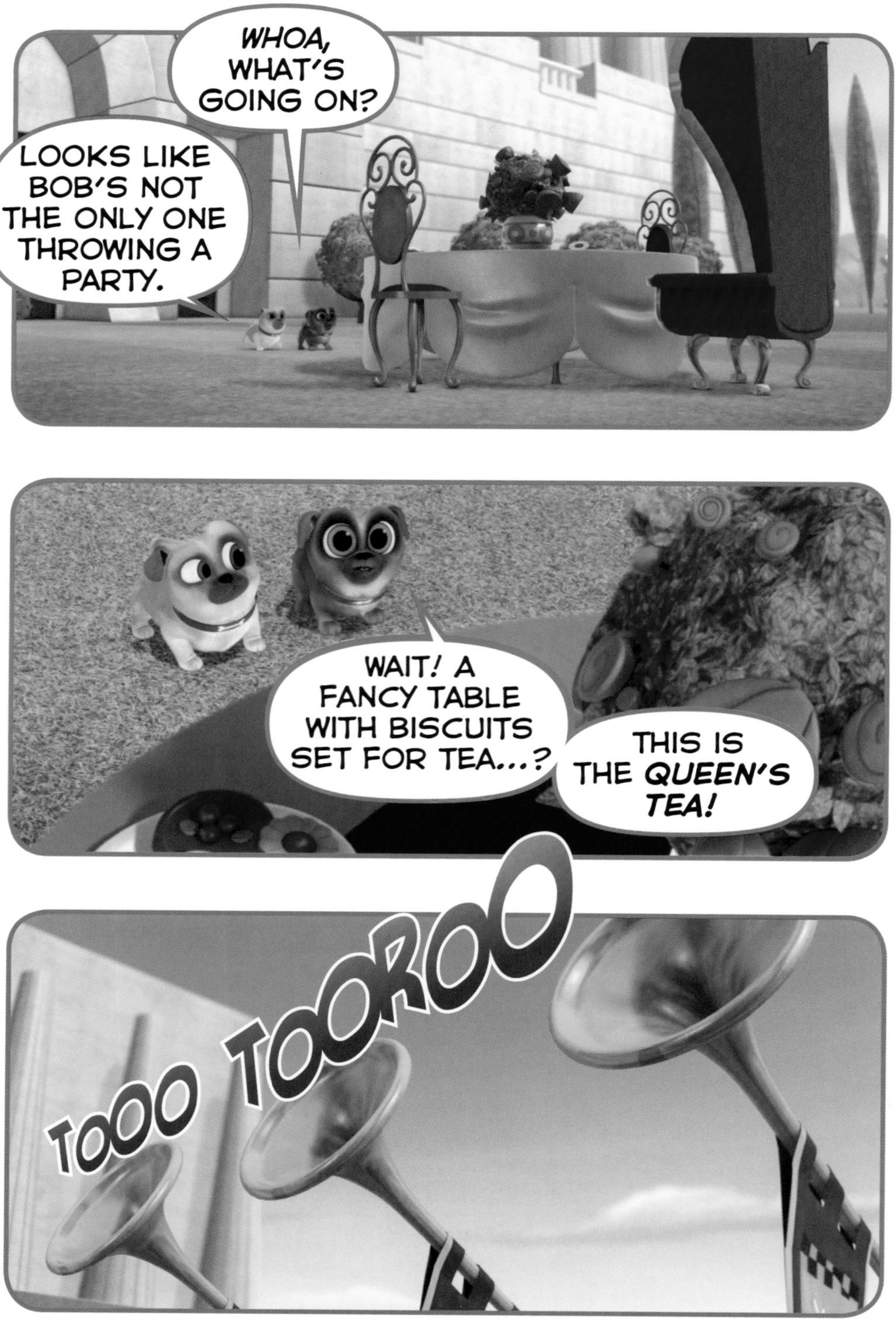
WHOA, WHAT'S GOING ON?
LOOKS LIKE BOB'S NOT THE ONLY ONE THROWING A PARTY.
WAIT! A FANCY TABLE WITH BISCUITS SET FOR TEA...?
THIS IS THE QUEEN'S TEA!
TOOO TOOROO

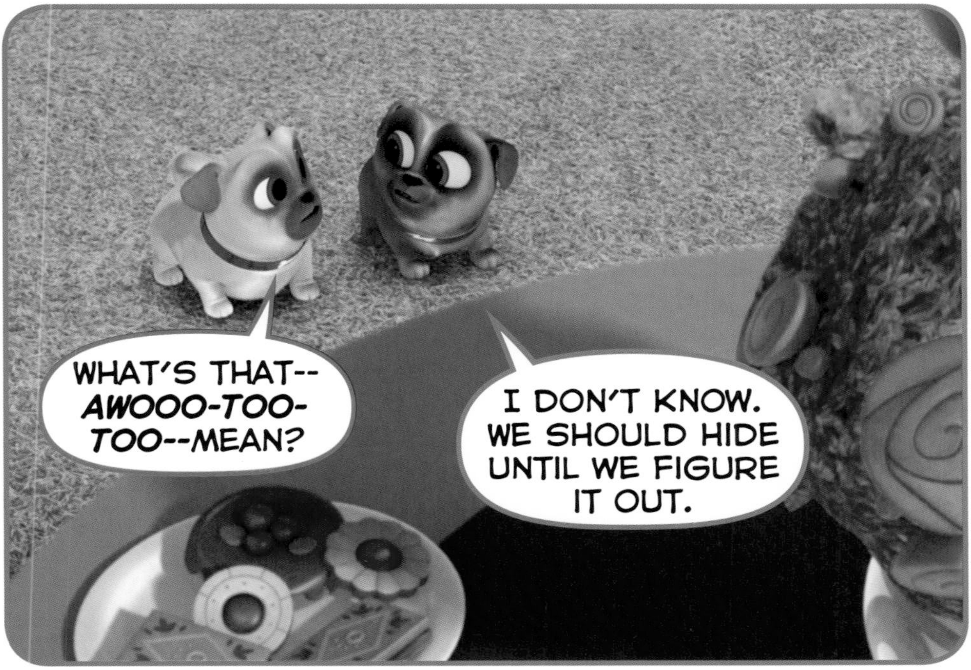
WHAT'S THAT--*AWOOO-TOO-TOO*--MEAN?
I DON'T KNOW. WE SHOULD HIDE UNTIL WE FIGURE IT OUT.

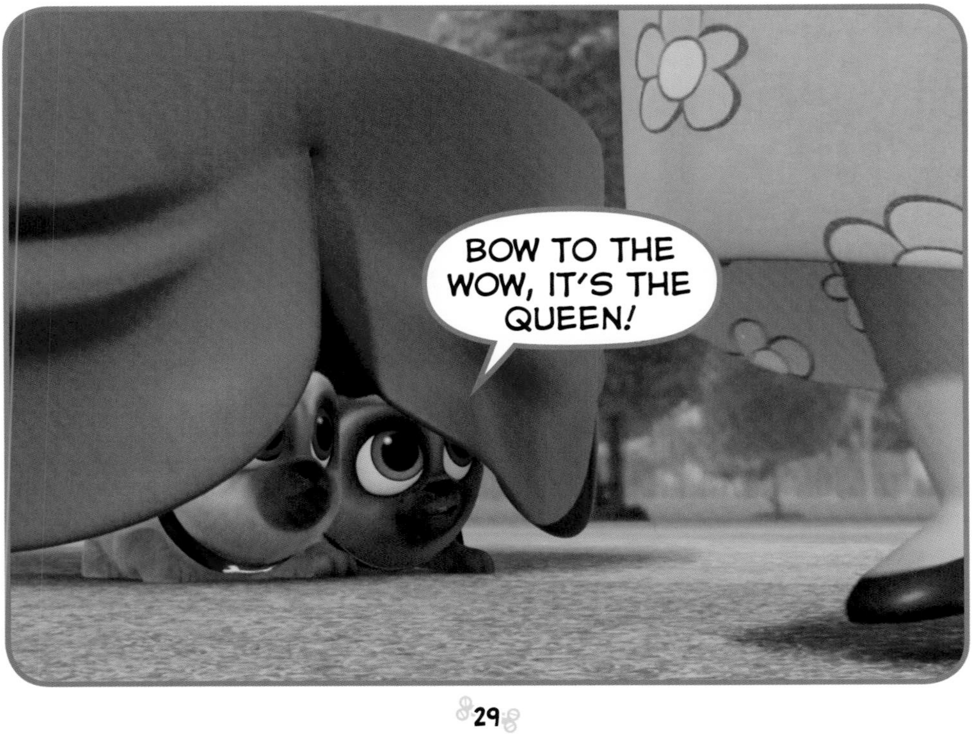
BOW TO THE WOW, IT'S THE QUEEN!

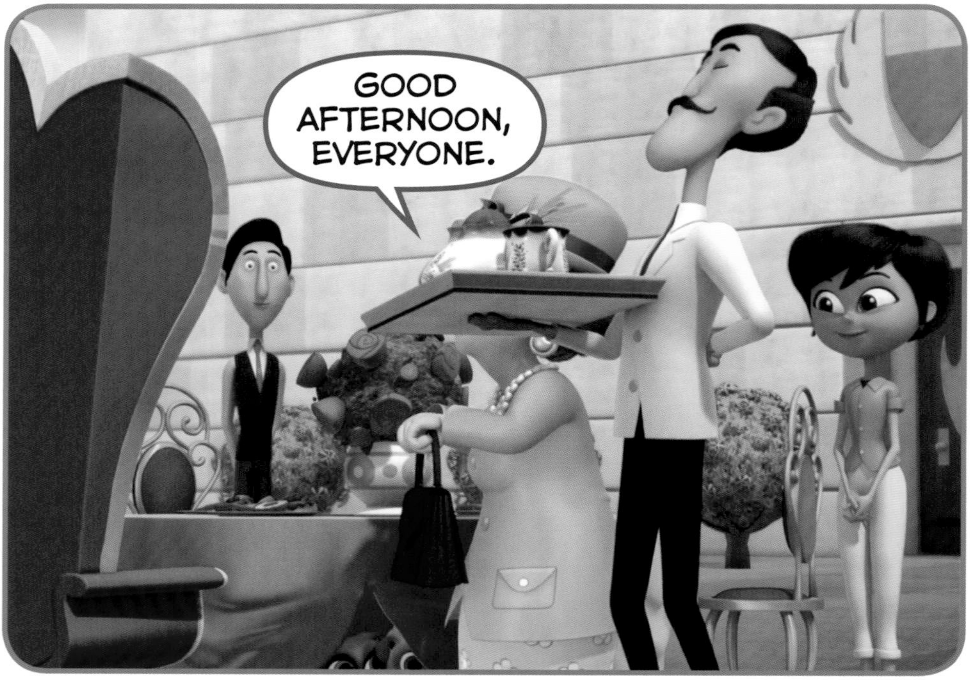
GOOD AFTERNOON, EVERYONE.

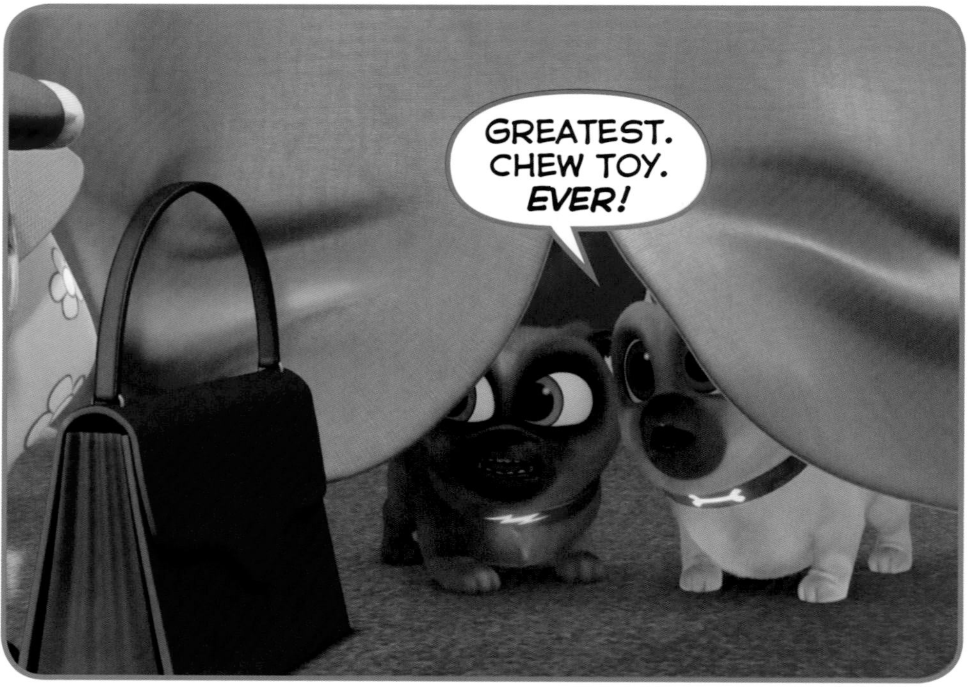
GREATEST. CHEW TOY. *EVER!*

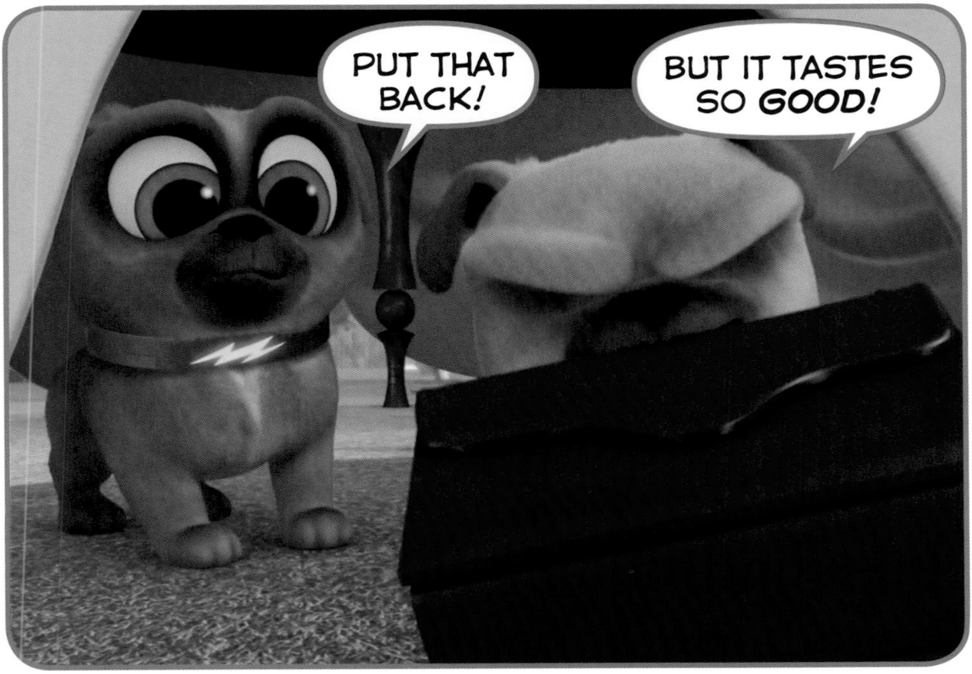
PUT THAT BACK!
BUT IT TASTES SO GOOD!

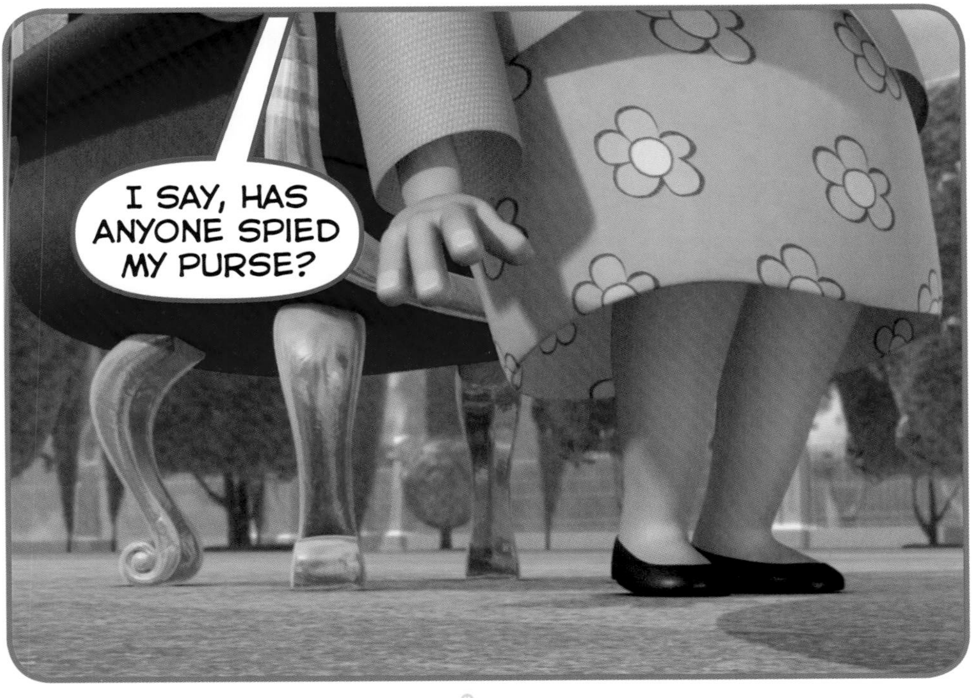
I SAY, HAS ANYONE SPIED MY PURSE?

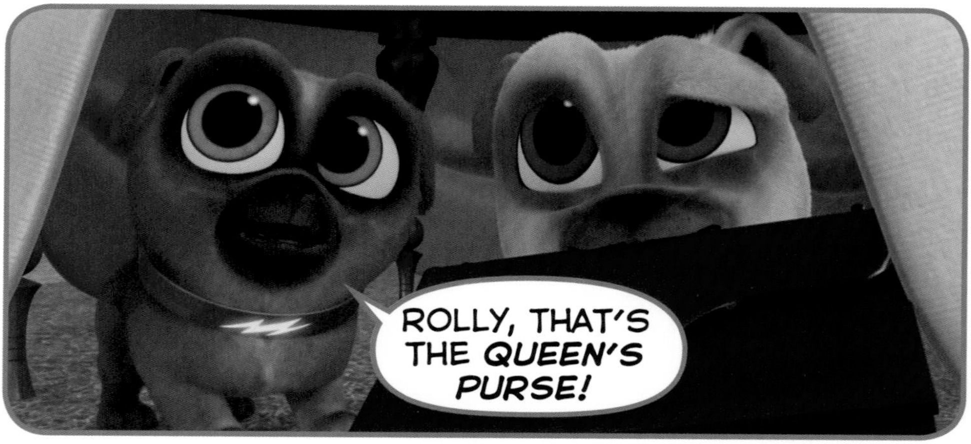
ROLLY, THAT'S THE *QUEEN'S* *PURSE!*

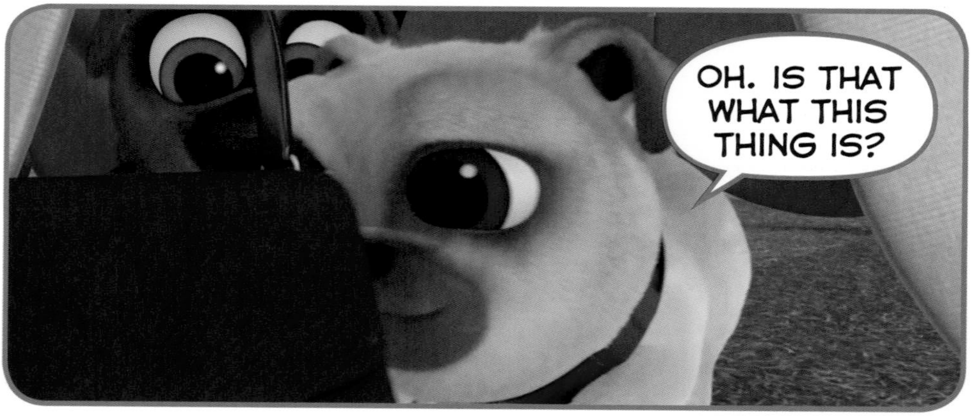
OH. IS THAT WHAT THIS THING IS?

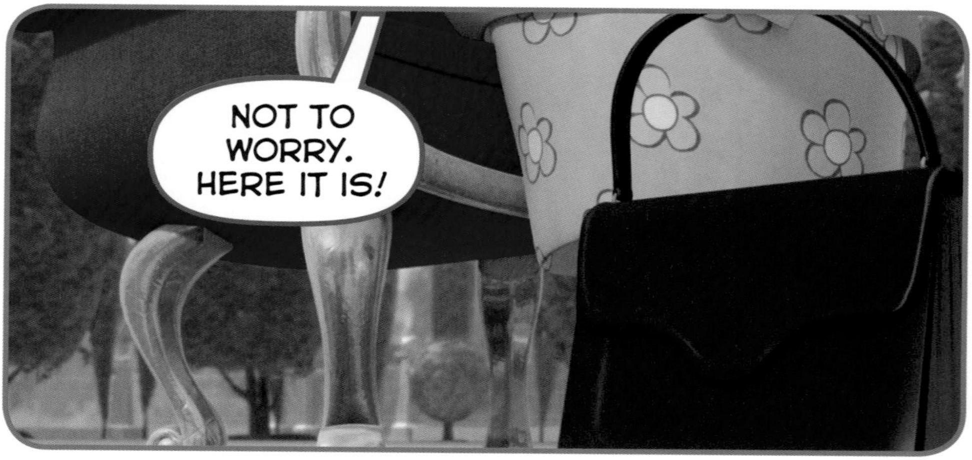
NOT TO WORRY. HERE IT IS!

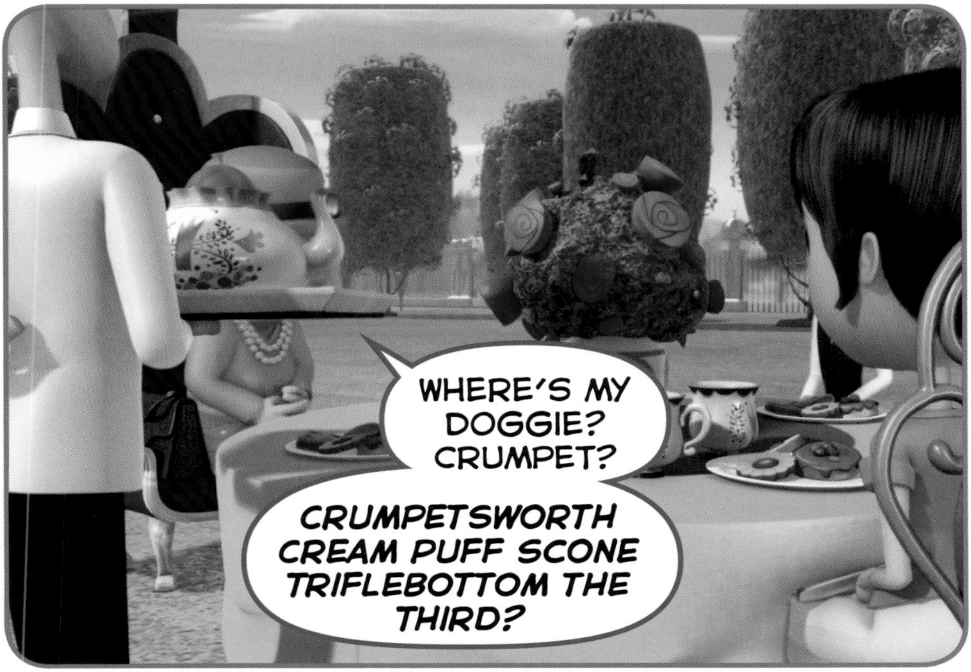
WHERE'S MY DOGGIE? CRUMPET?
CRUMPETSWORTH CREAM PUFF SCONE TRIFLEBOTTOM THE THIRD?

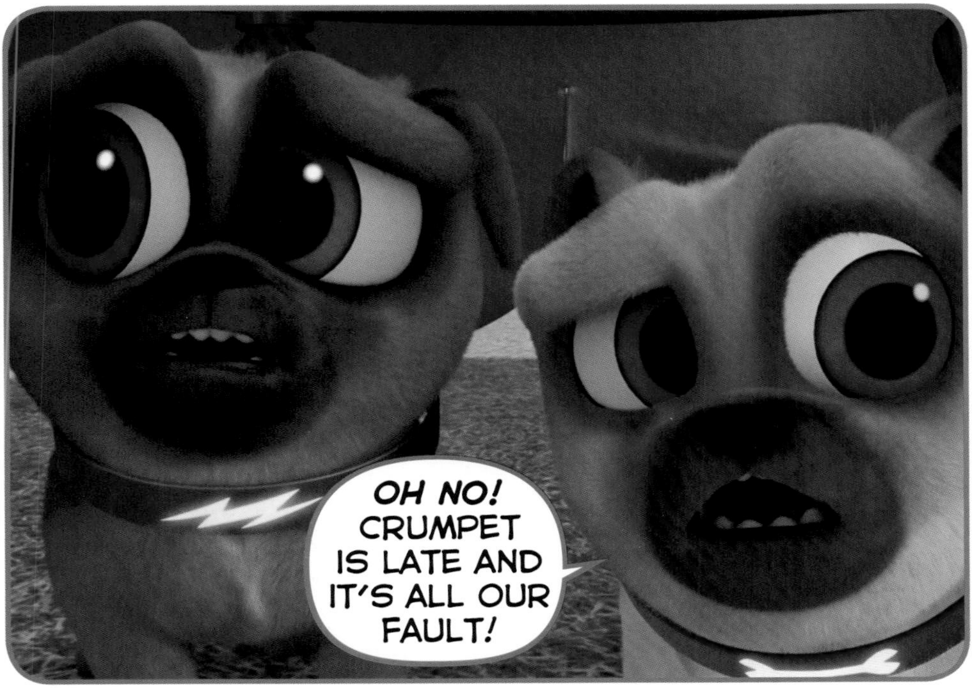
OH NO! CRUMPET IS LATE AND IT'S ALL OUR FAULT!

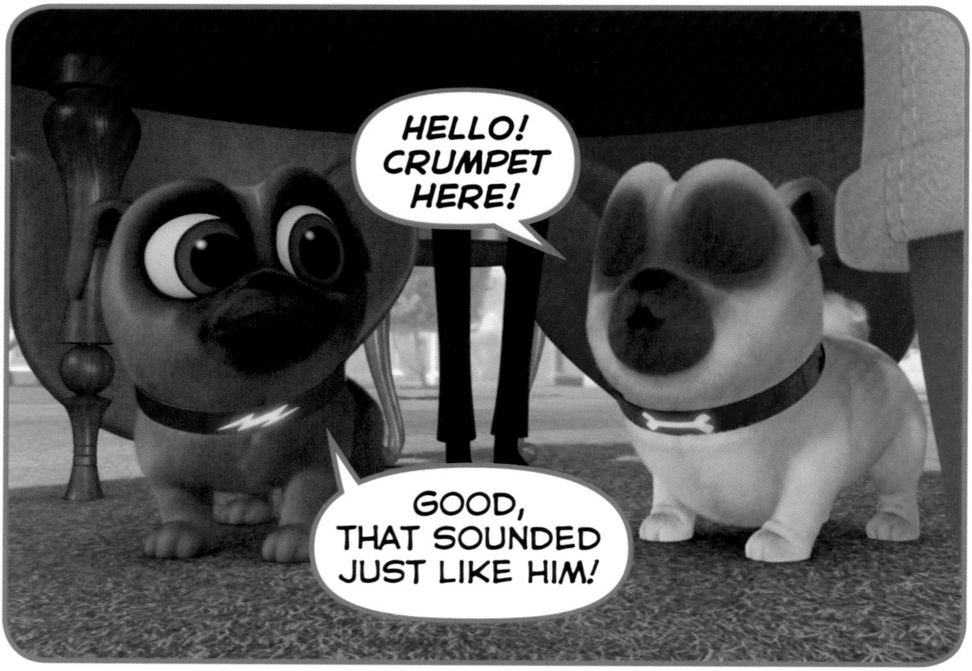
HELLO! CRUMPET HERE!
GOOD, THAT SOUNDED JUST LIKE HIM!

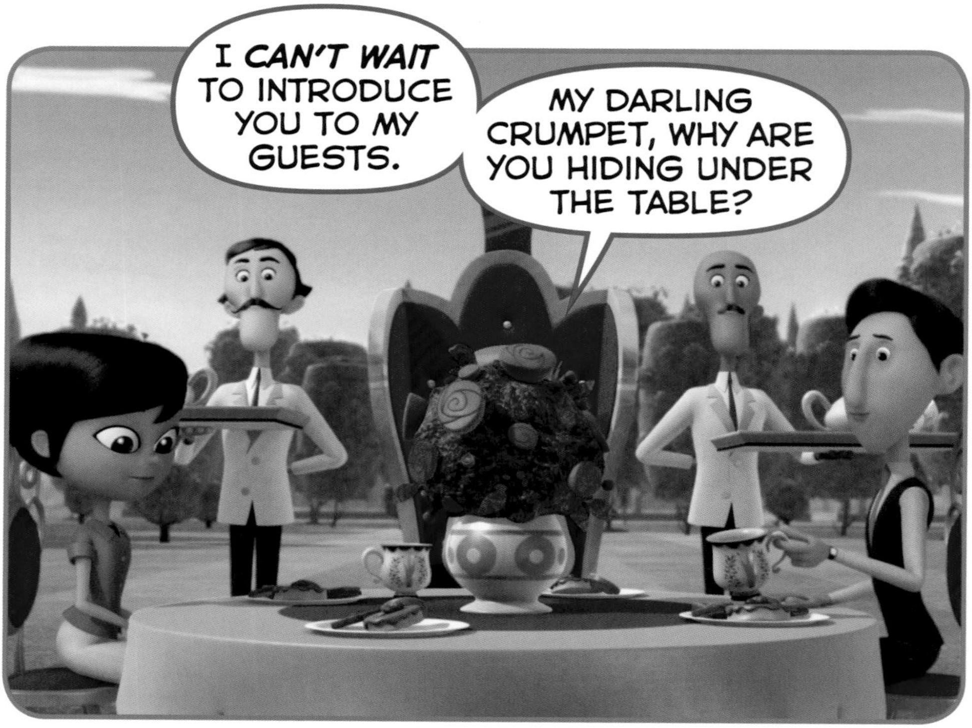
I CAN'T WAIT TO INTRODUCE YOU TO MY GUESTS.
MY DARLING CRUMPET, WHY ARE YOU HIDING UNDER THE TABLE?

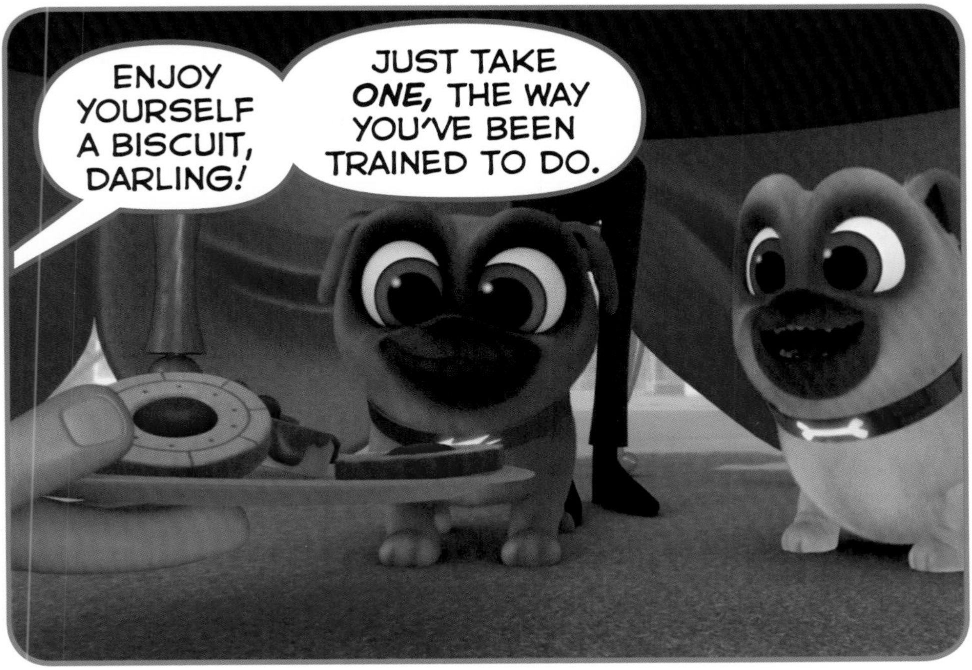
ENJOY YOURSELF A BISCUIT, DARLING!
JUST TAKE *ONE,* THE WAY YOU'VE BEEN TRAINED TO DO.

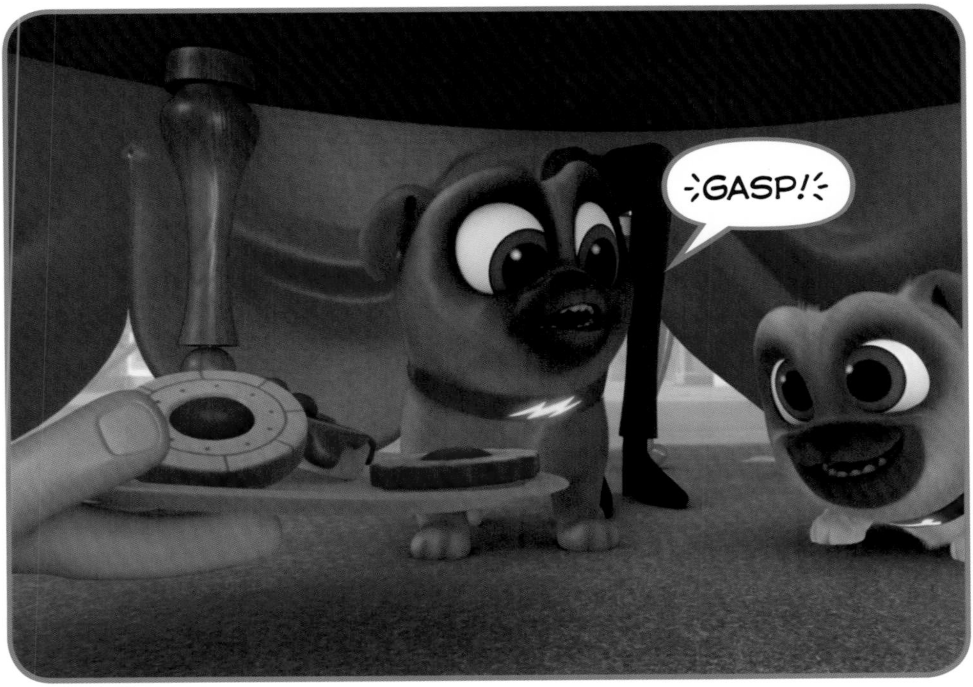
GASP!

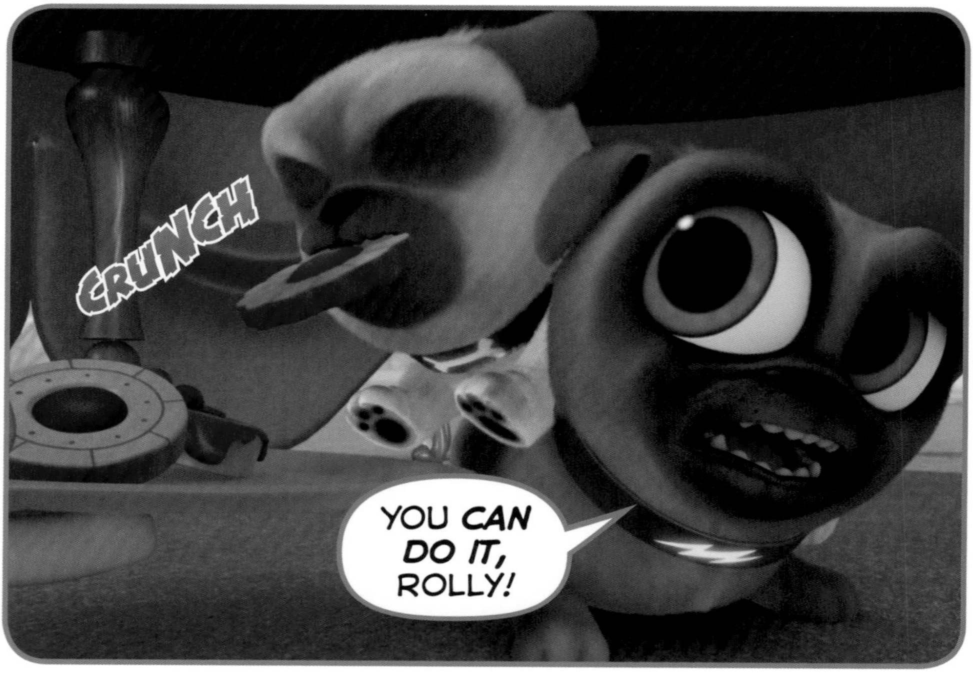
CRUNCH
YOU CAN DO IT, ROLLY!

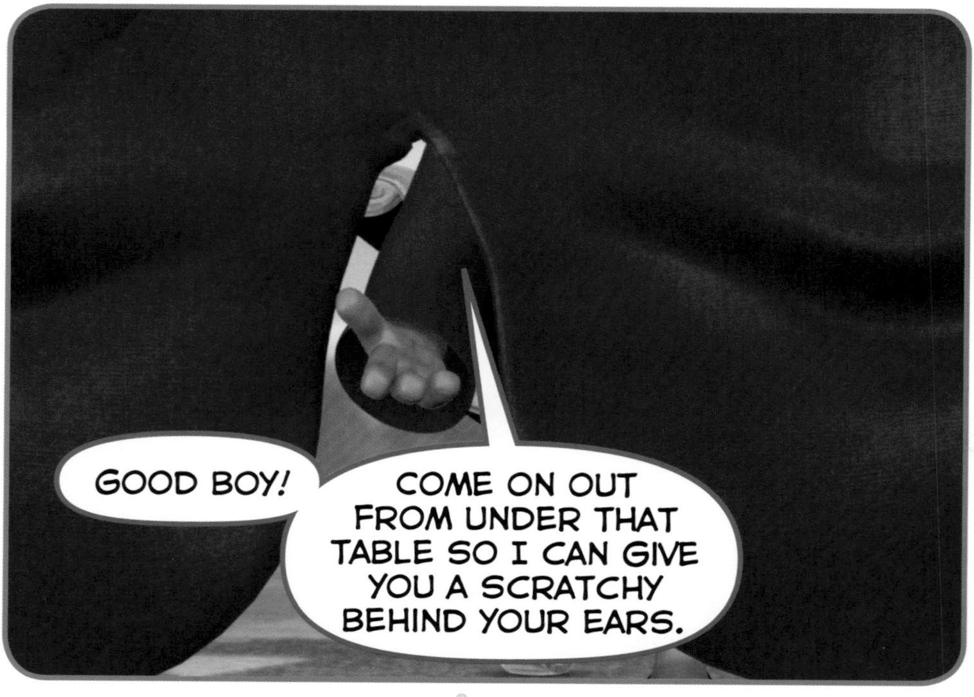
GOOD BOY!
COME ON OUT FROM UNDER THAT TABLE SO I CAN GIVE YOU A SCRATCHY BEHIND YOUR EARS.

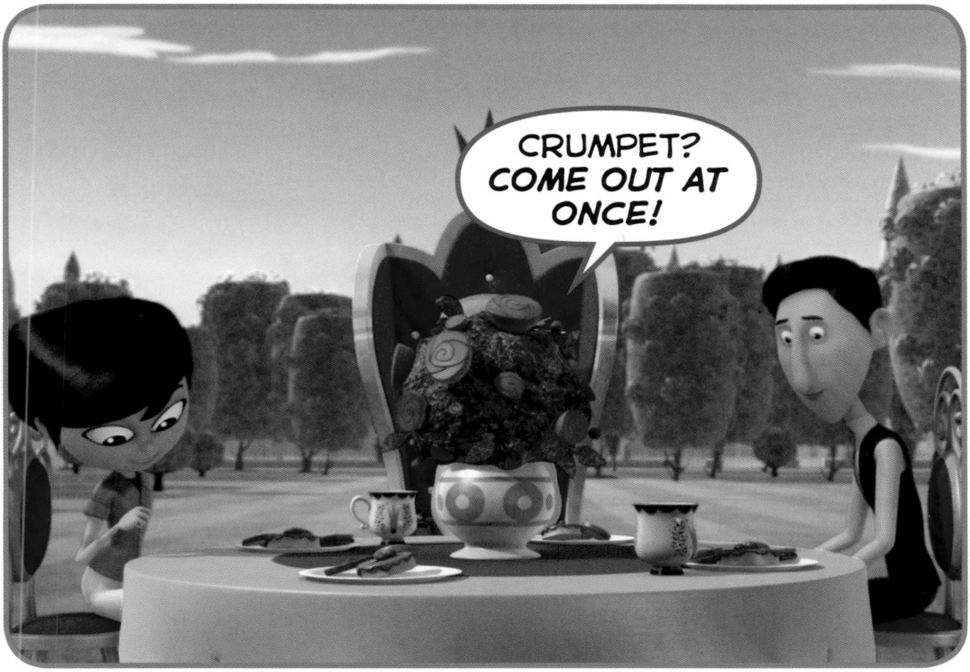
CRUMPET? COME OUT AT ONCE!

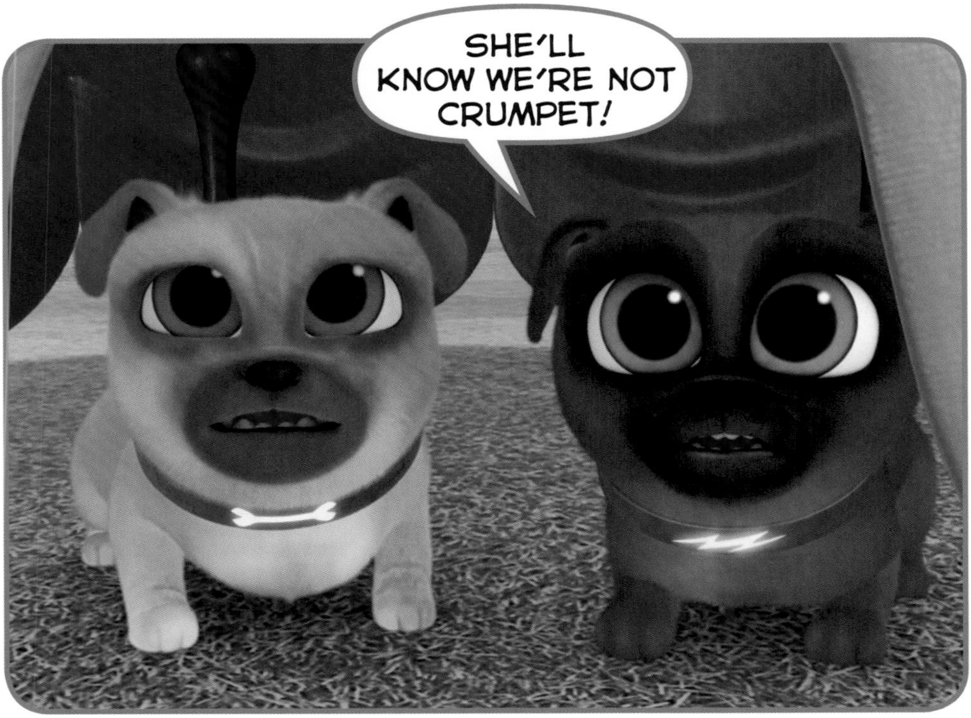
SHE'LL KNOW WE'RE NOT CRUMPET!

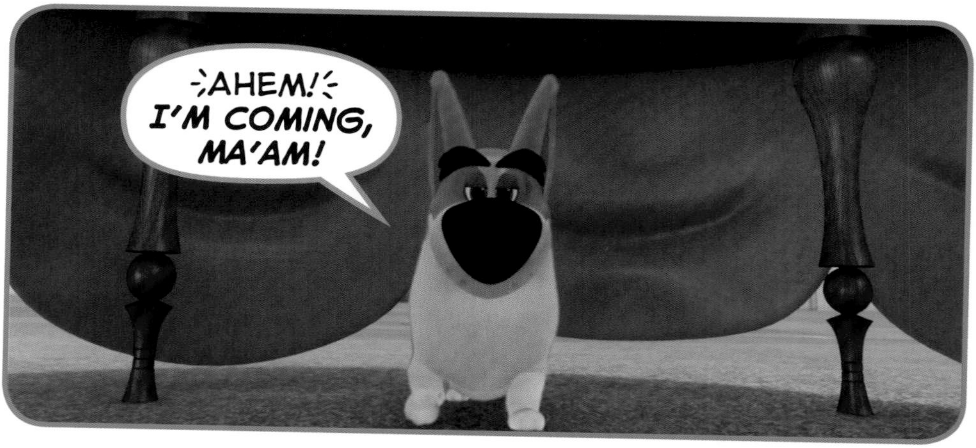
AHEM!
I'M COMING, MA'AM!

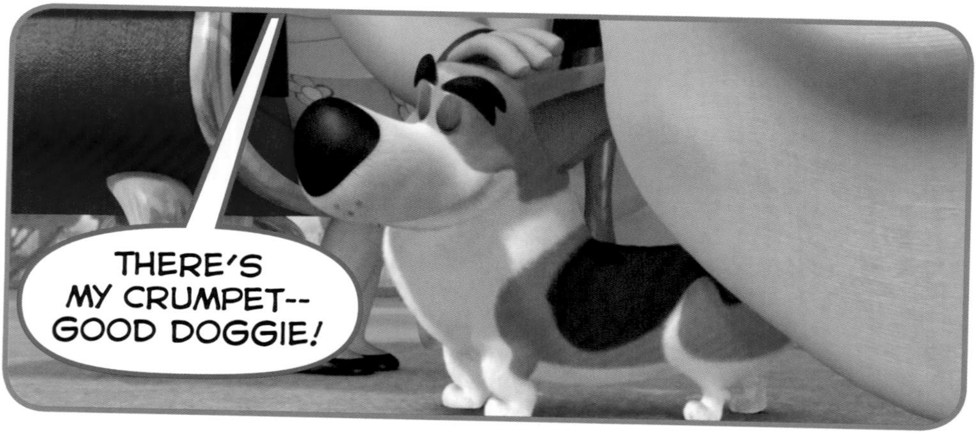
THERE'S MY CRUMPET-- GOOD DOGGIE!

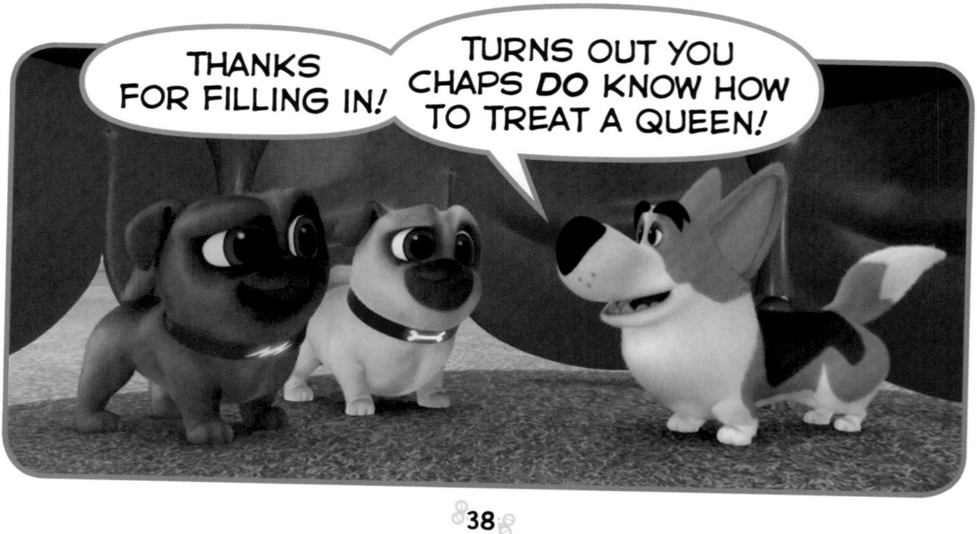
THANKS FOR FILLING IN!
TURNS OUT YOU CHAPS DO KNOW HOW TO TREAT A QUEEN!

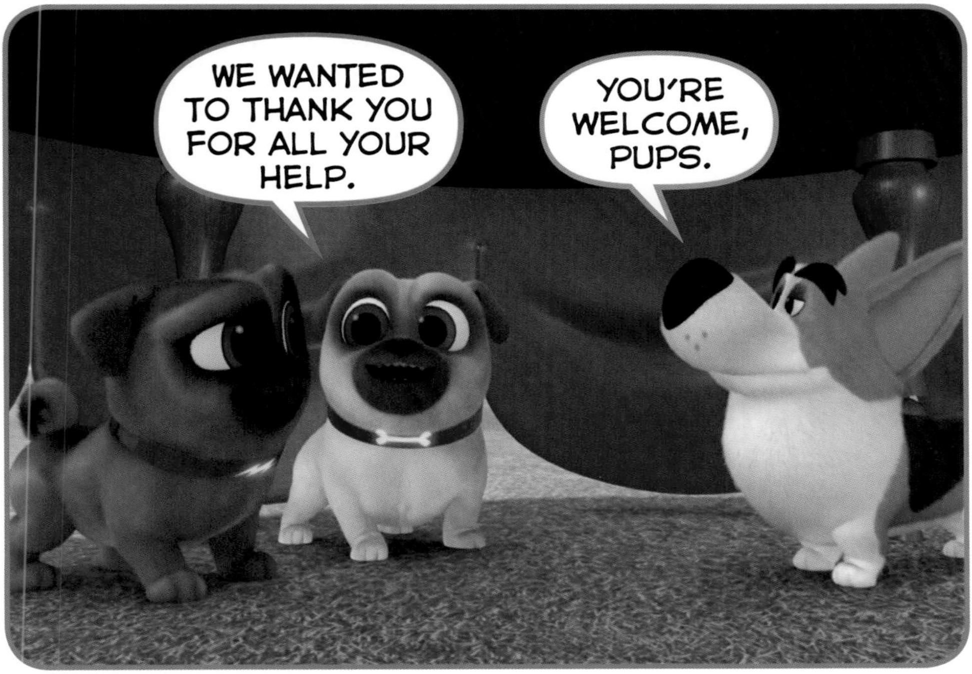
WE WANTED TO THANK YOU FOR ALL YOUR HELP.
YOU'RE WELCOME, PUPS.

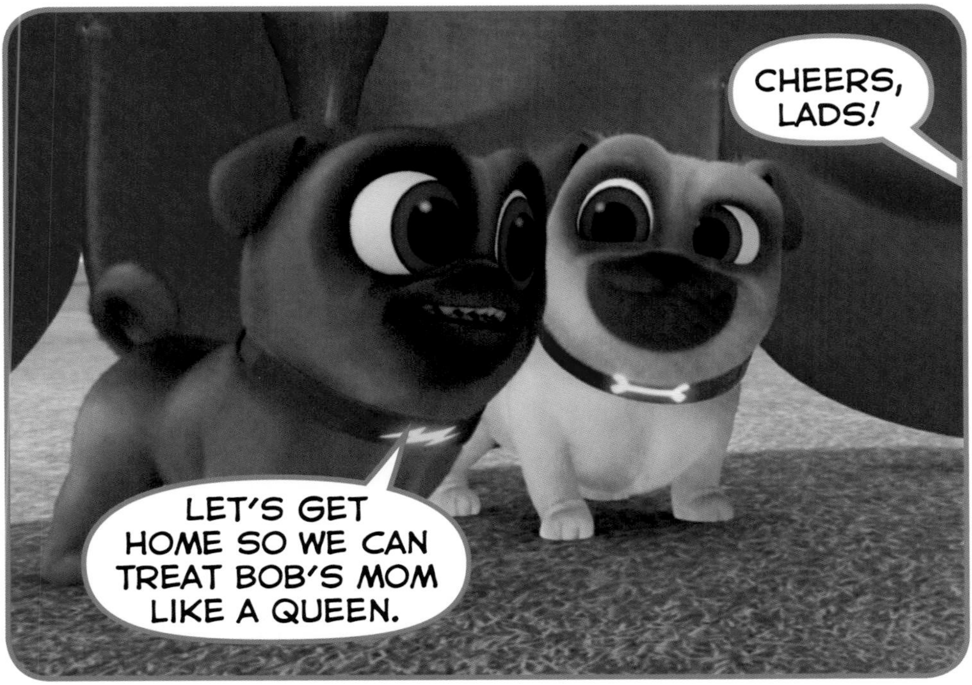
CHEERS, LADS!
LET'S GET HOME SO WE CAN TREAT BOB'S MOM LIKE A QUEEN.

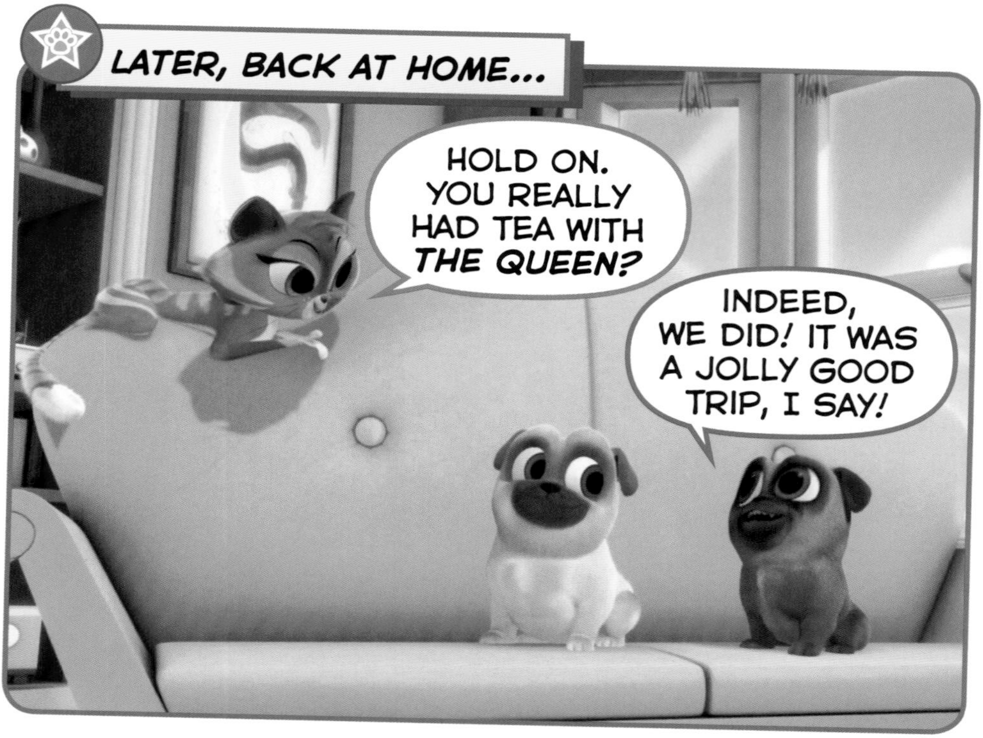
LATER, BACK AT HOME...
HOLD ON. YOU REALLY HAD TEA WITH THE QUEEN?
INDEED, WE DID! IT WAS A JOLLY GOOD TRIP, I SAY!

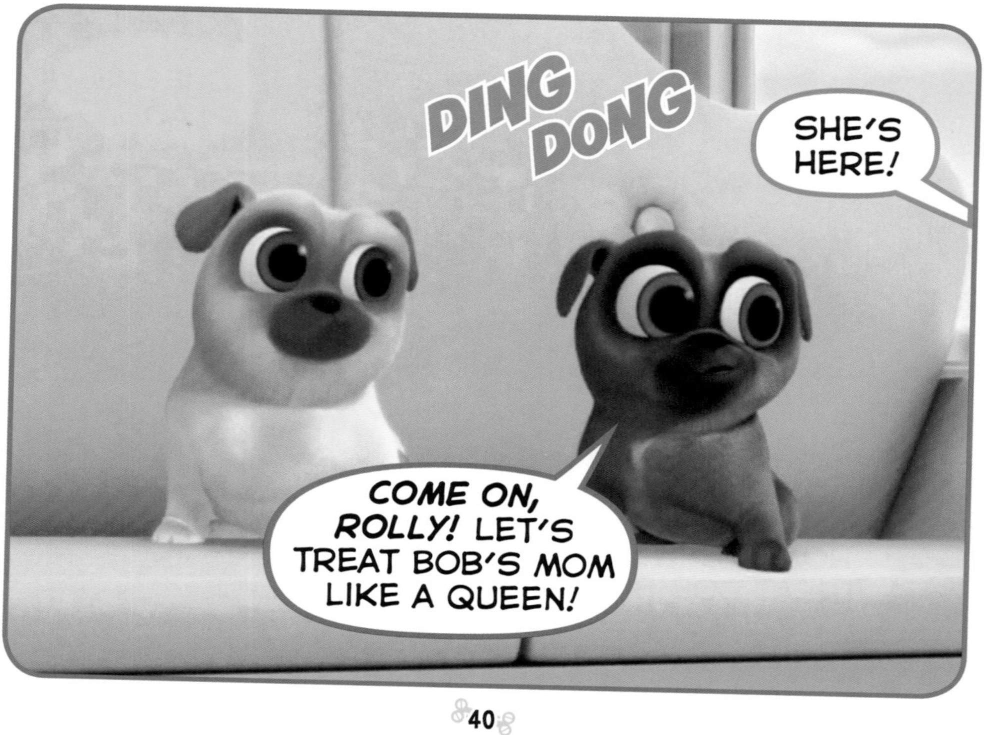
DING DONG
SHE'S HERE!
COME ON, ROLLY! LET'S TREAT BOB'S MOM LIKE A QUEEN!

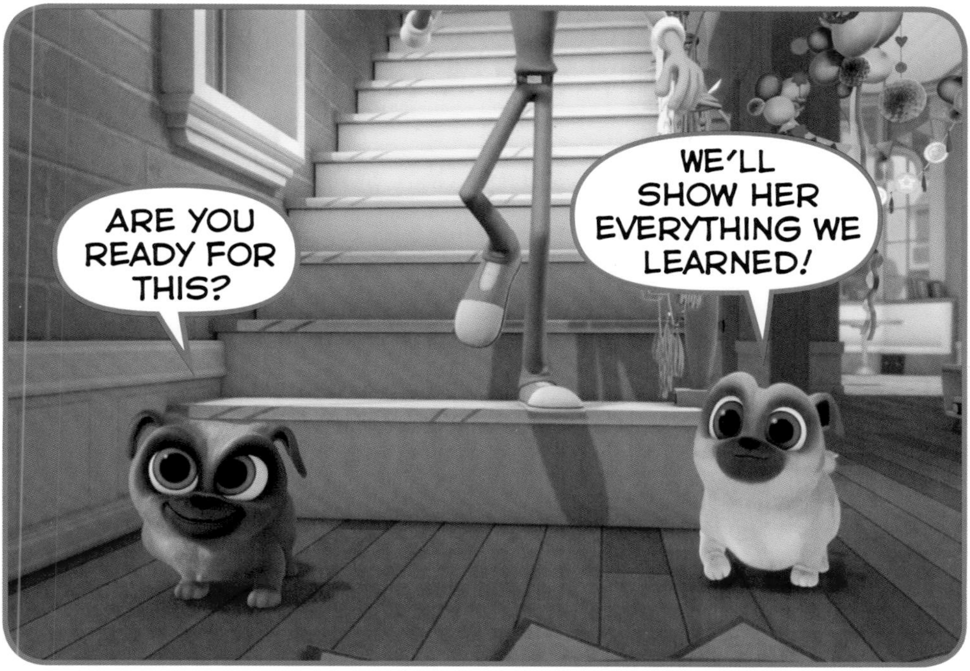
ARE YOU READY FOR THIS?
WE'LL SHOW HER EVERYTHING WE LEARNED!

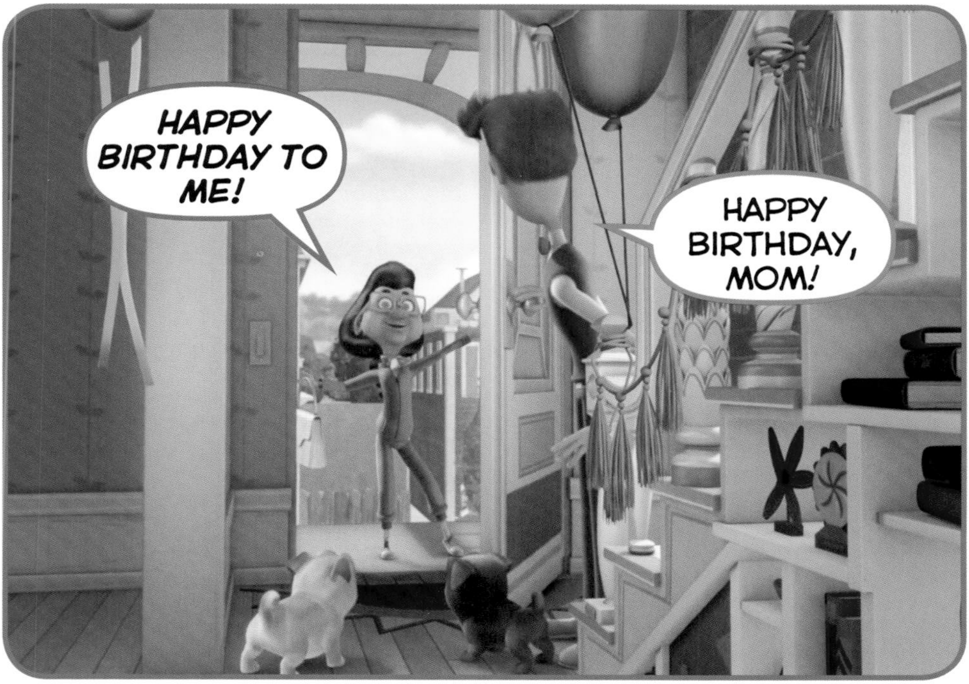
HAPPY BIRTHDAY TO ME!
HAPPY BIRTHDAY, MOM!

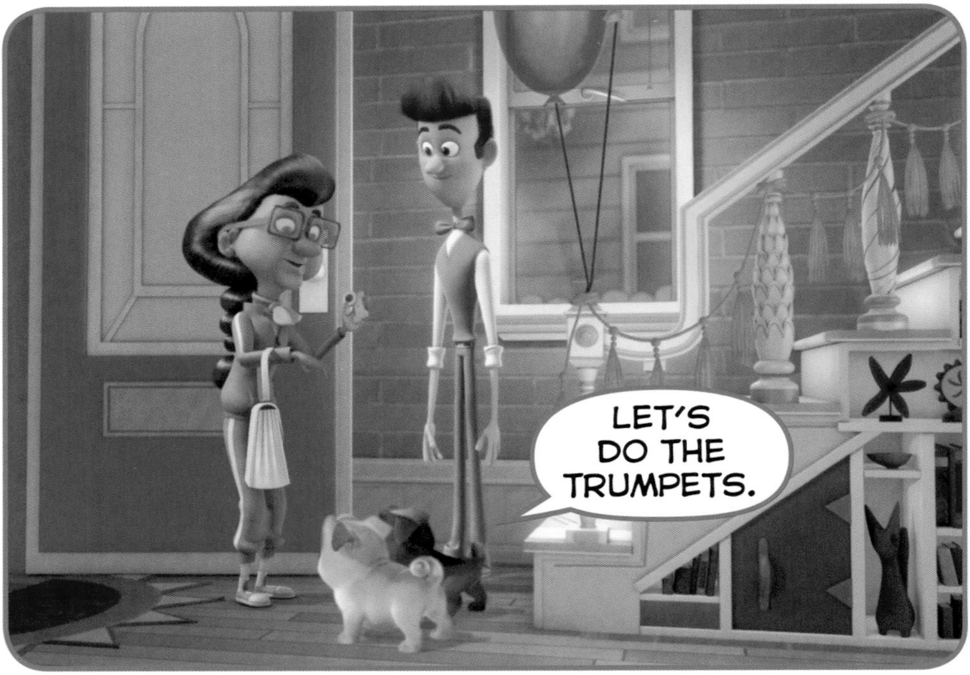
LET'S DO THE TRUMPETS.

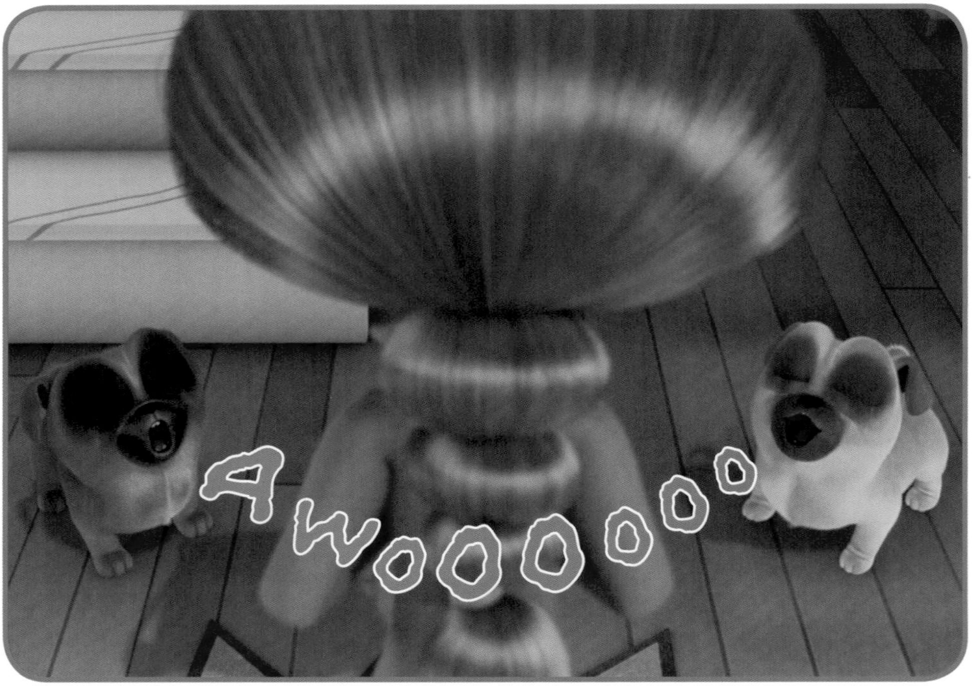
AWOOOOOO

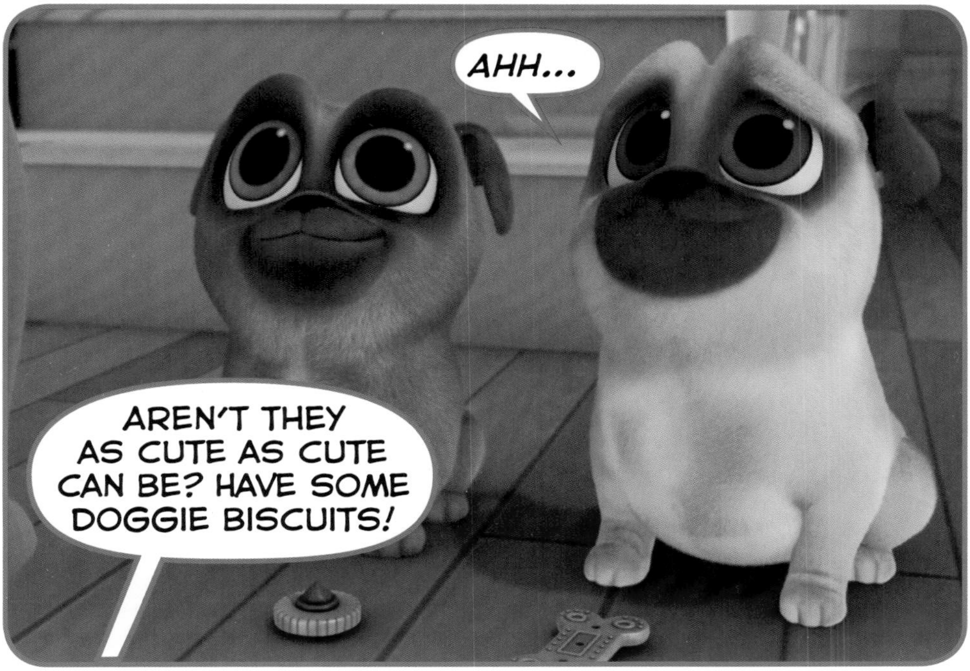
AHH...
AREN'T THEY AS CUTE AS CUTE CAN BE? HAVE SOME DOGGIE BISCUITS!

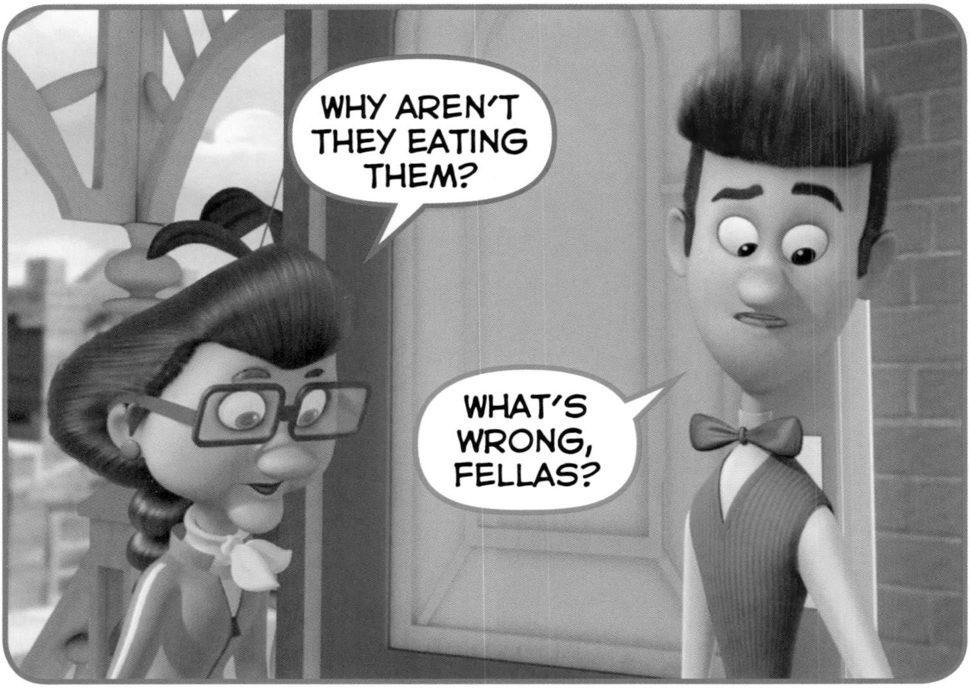
WHY AREN'T THEY EATING THEM?
WHAT'S WRONG, FELLAS?

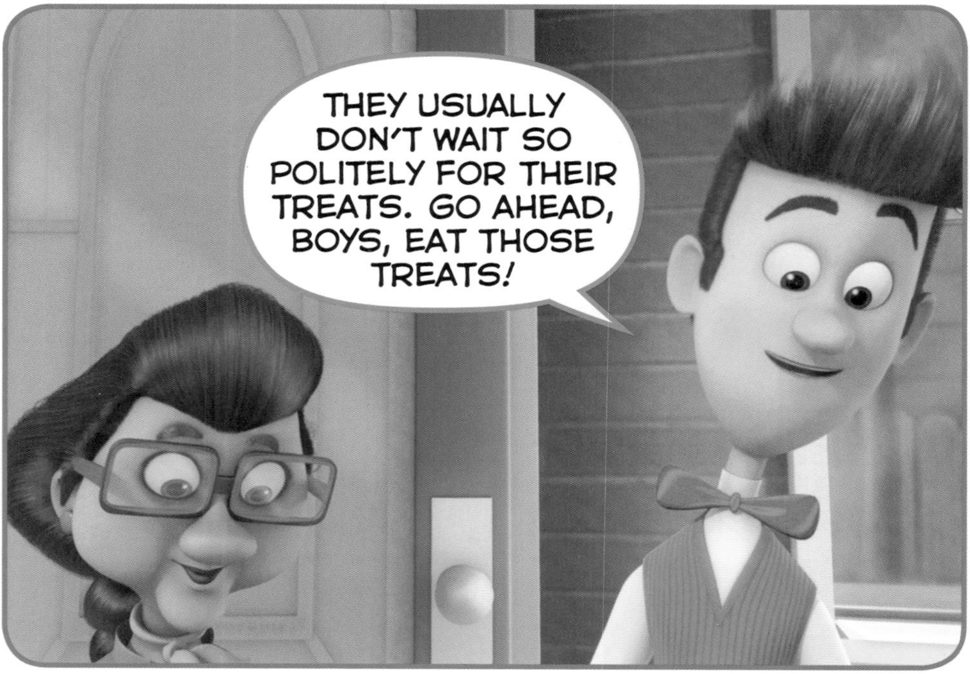
THEY USUALLY DON'T WAIT SO POLITELY FOR THEIR TREATS. GO AHEAD, BOYS, EAT THOSE TREATS!

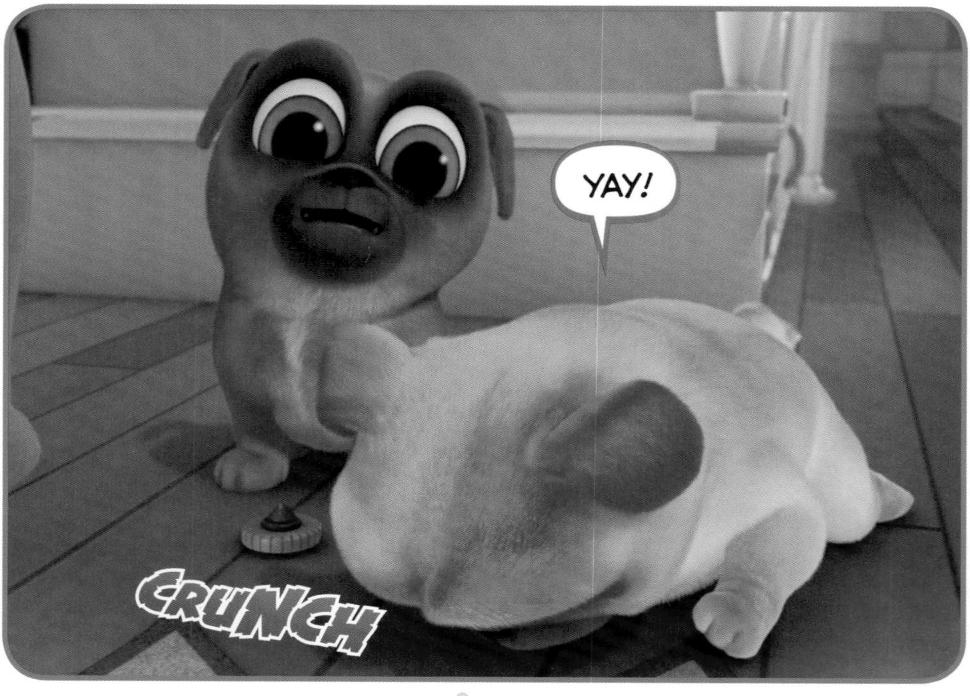
YAY!
CRUNCH

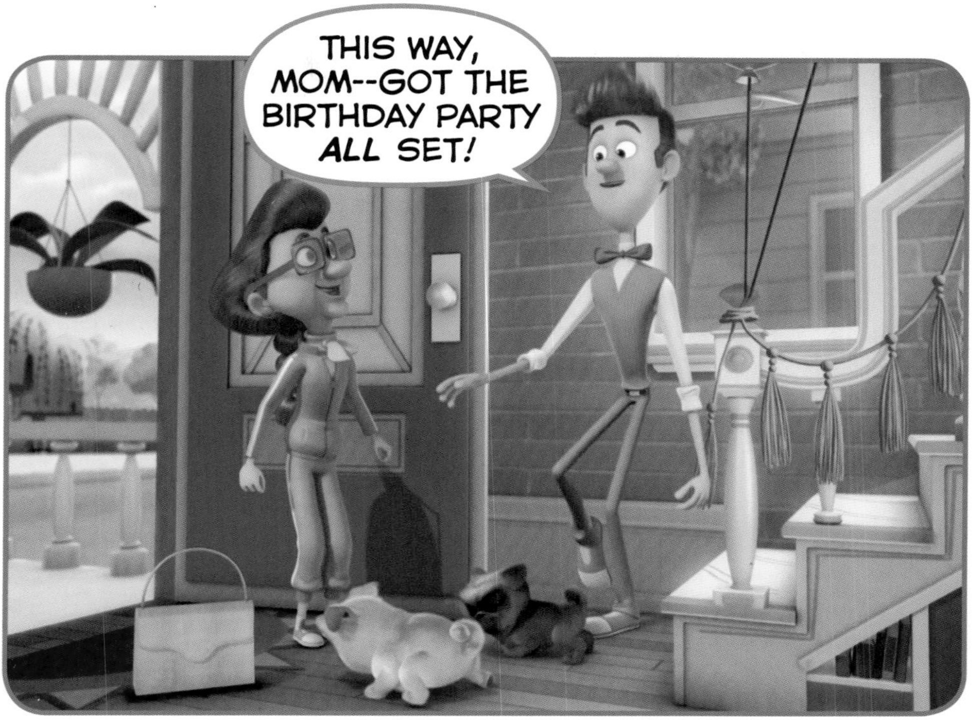
THIS WAY, MOM--GOT THE BIRTHDAY PARTY ALL SET!

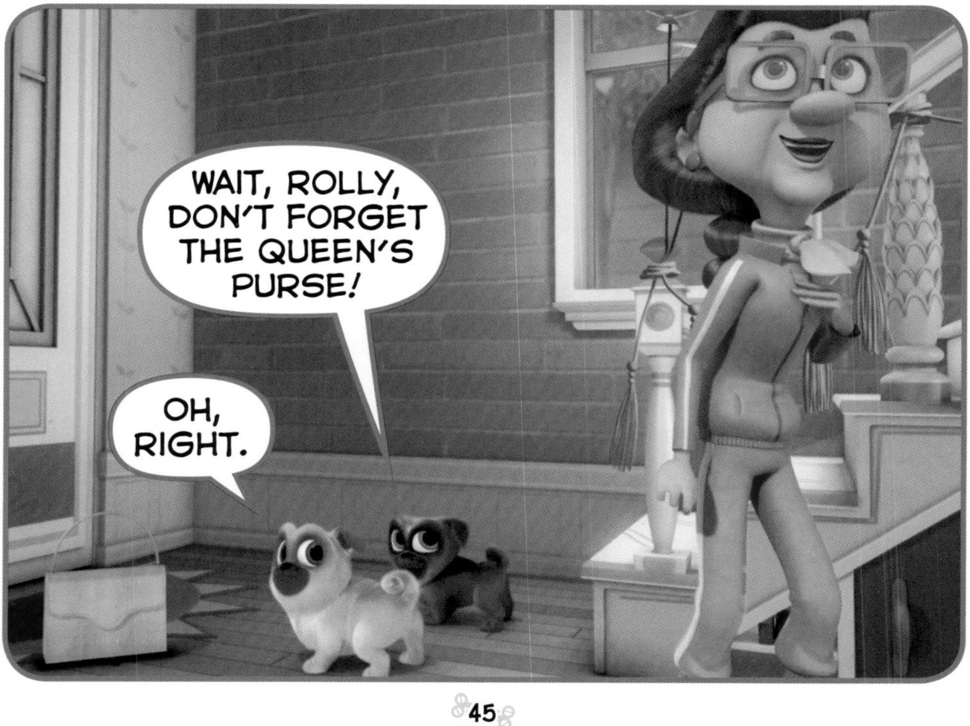
WAIT, ROLLY, DON'T FORGET THE QUEEN'S PURSE!
OH, RIGHT.

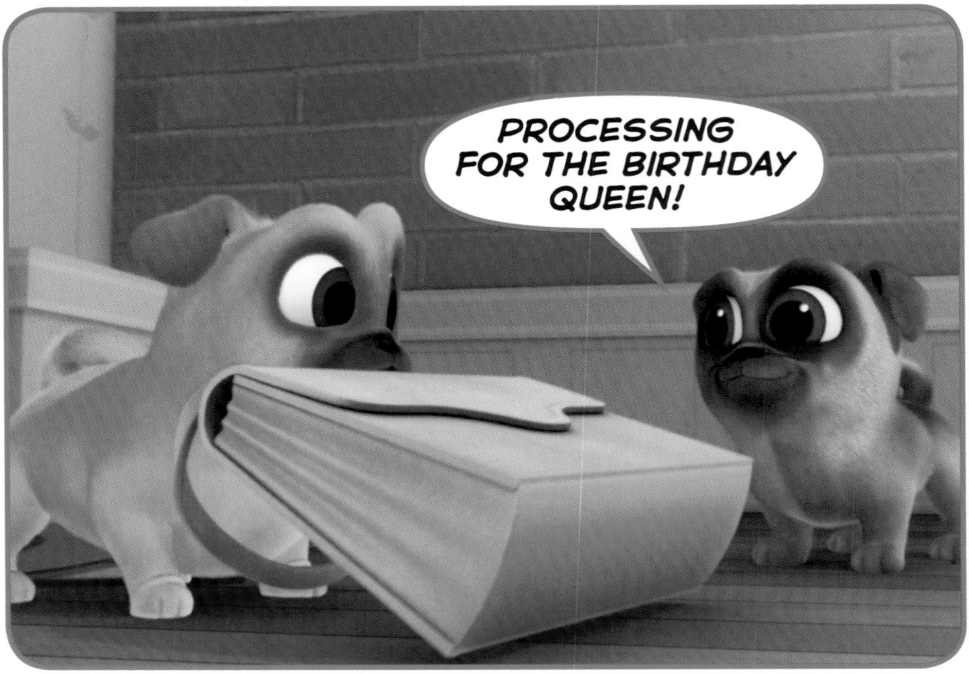
PROCESSING FOR THE BIRTHDAY QUEEN!

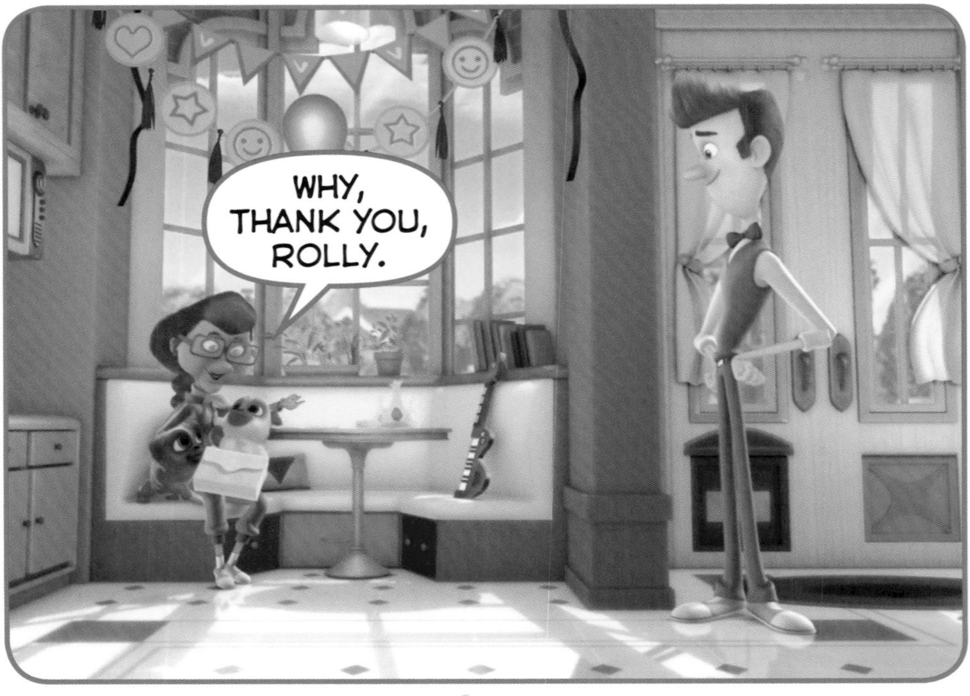
WHY, THANK YOU, ROLLY.

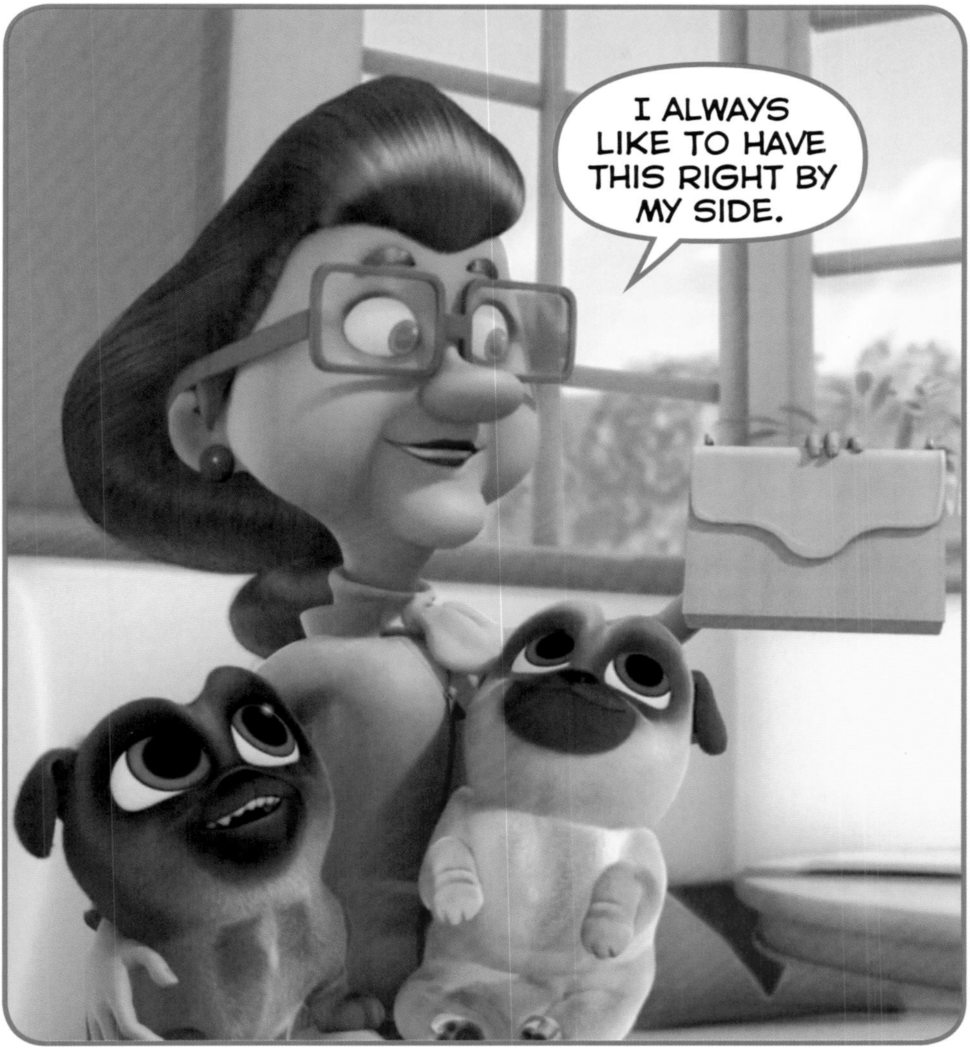
I ALWAYS LIKE TO HAVE THIS RIGHT BY MY SIDE.

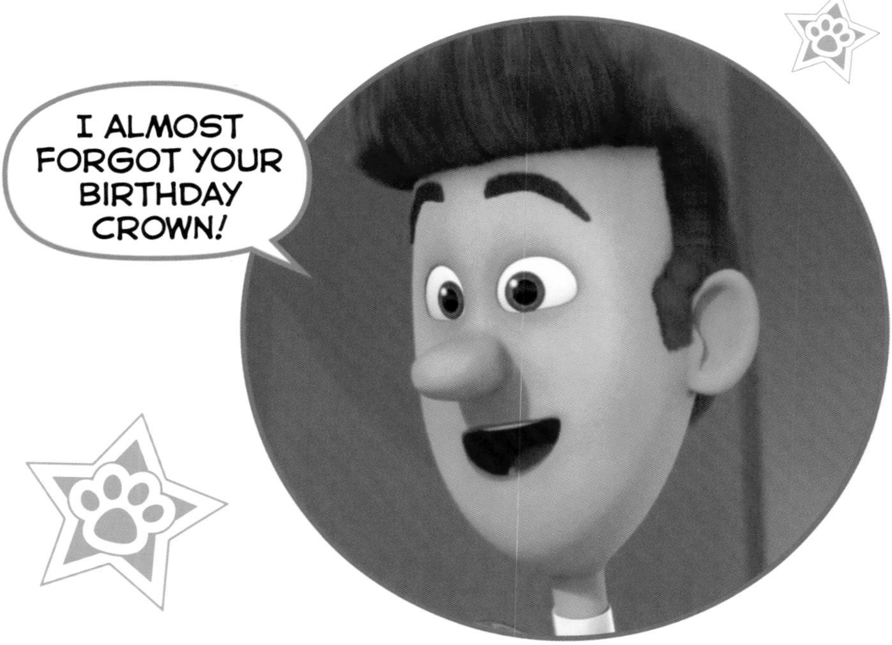
I ALMOST FORGOT YOUR BIRTHDAY CROWN!

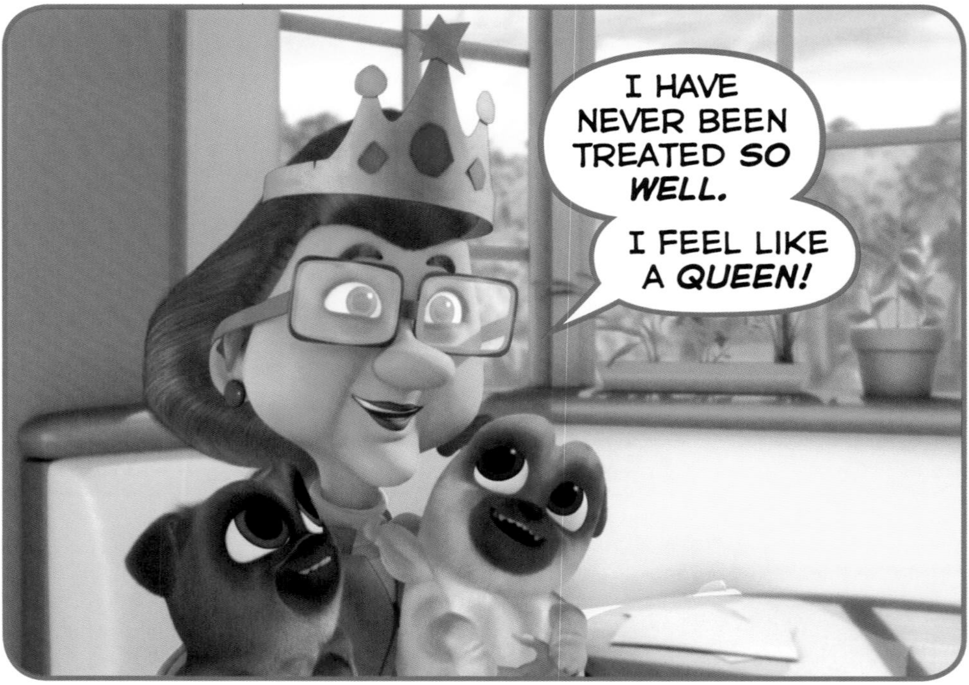
I HAVE NEVER BEEN TREATED SO *WELL.*
I FEEL LIKE A *QUEEN!*

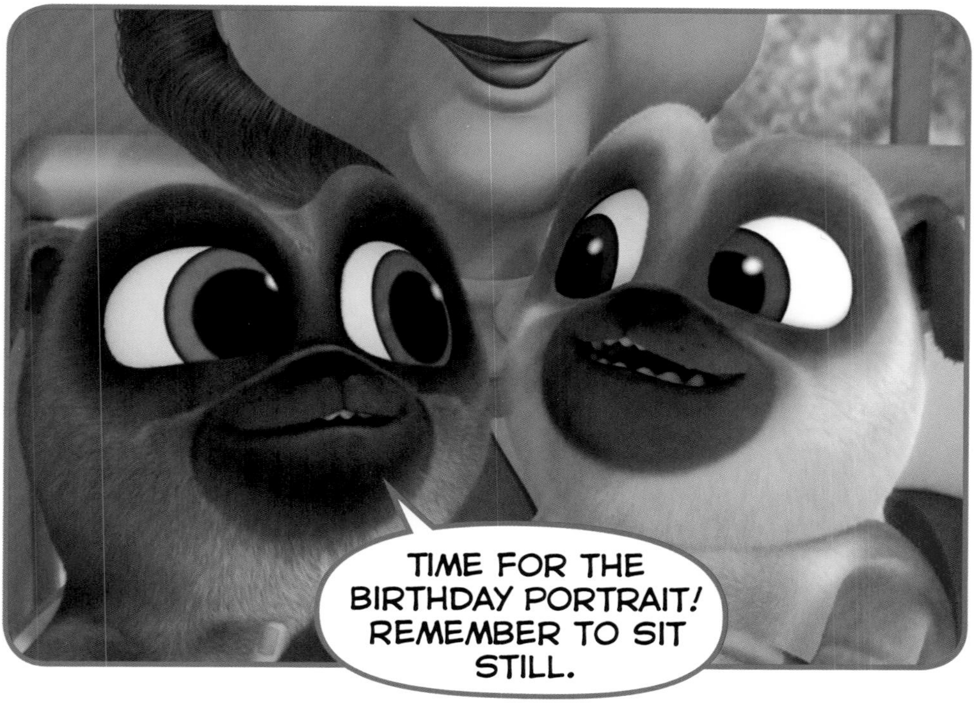
TIME FOR THE BIRTHDAY PORTRAIT! REMEMBER TO SIT STILL.

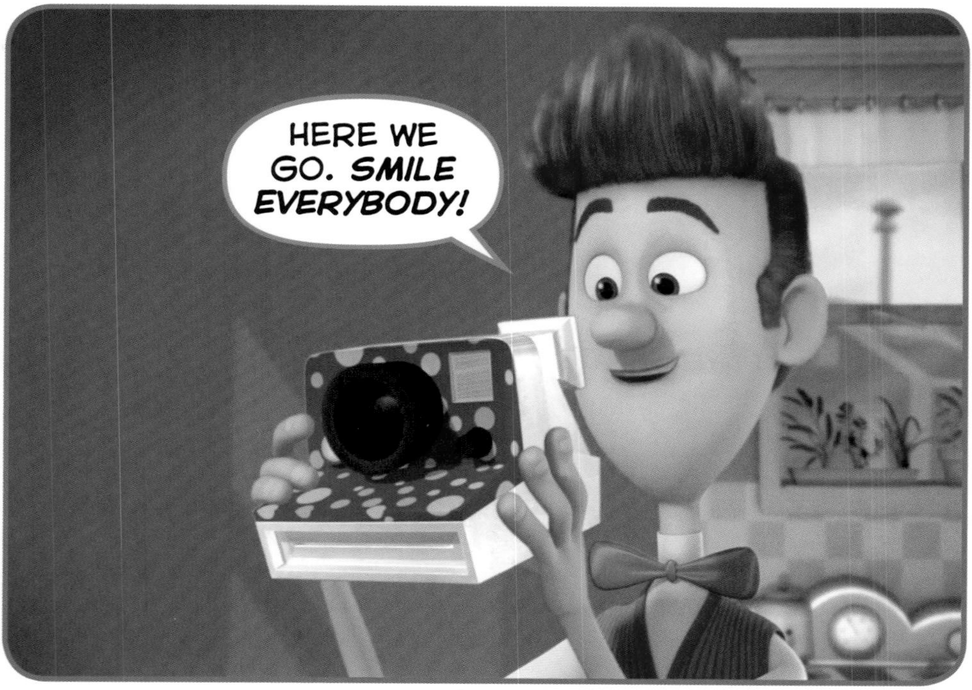
HERE WE GO. *SMILE EVERYBODY!*

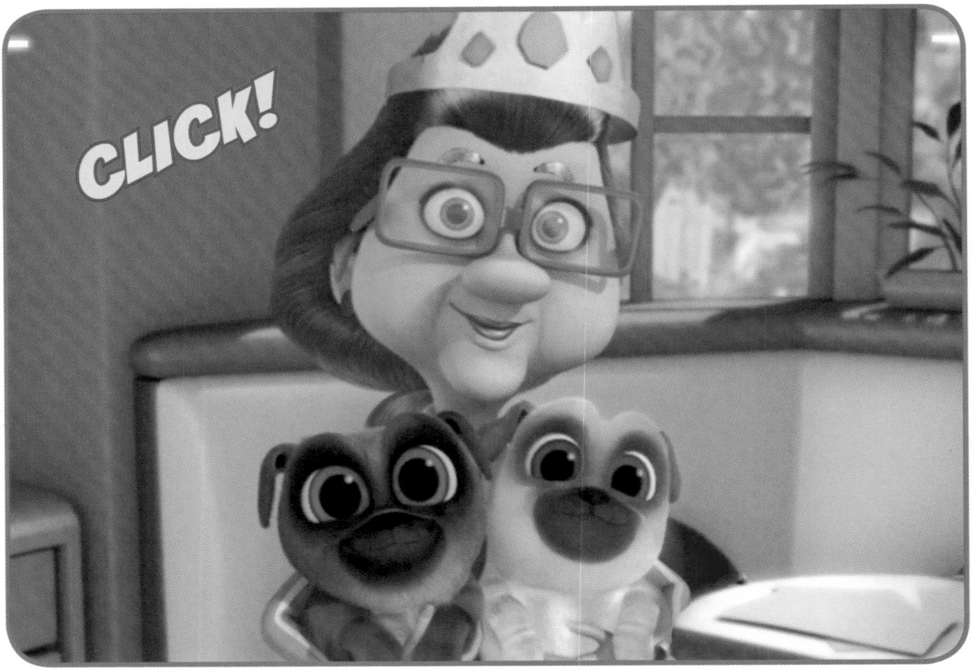
CLICK!

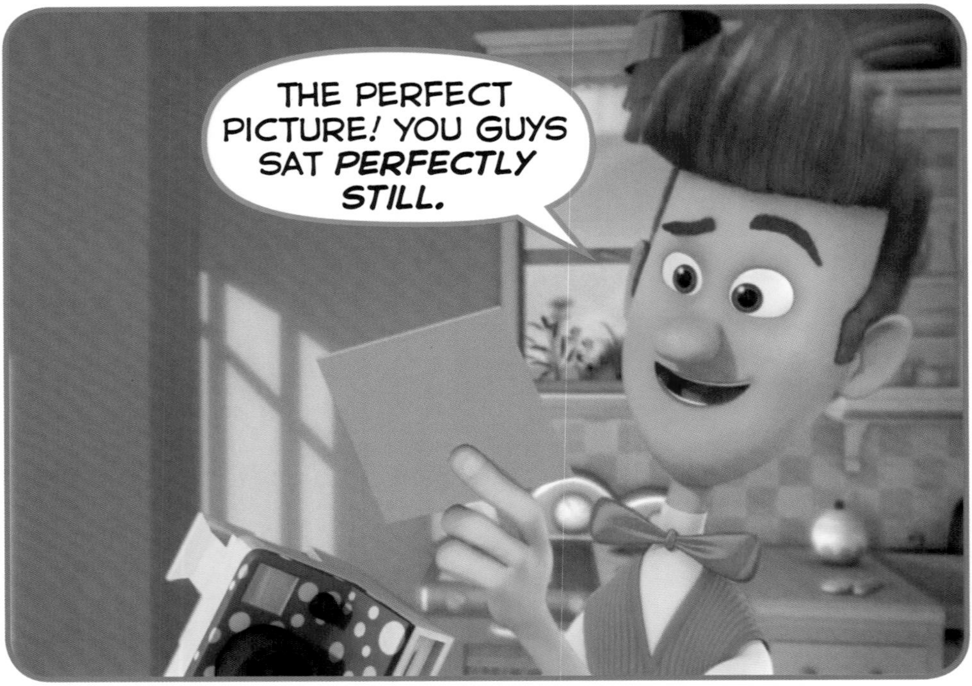
THE PERFECT PICTURE! YOU GUYS SAT *PERFECTLY STILL.*

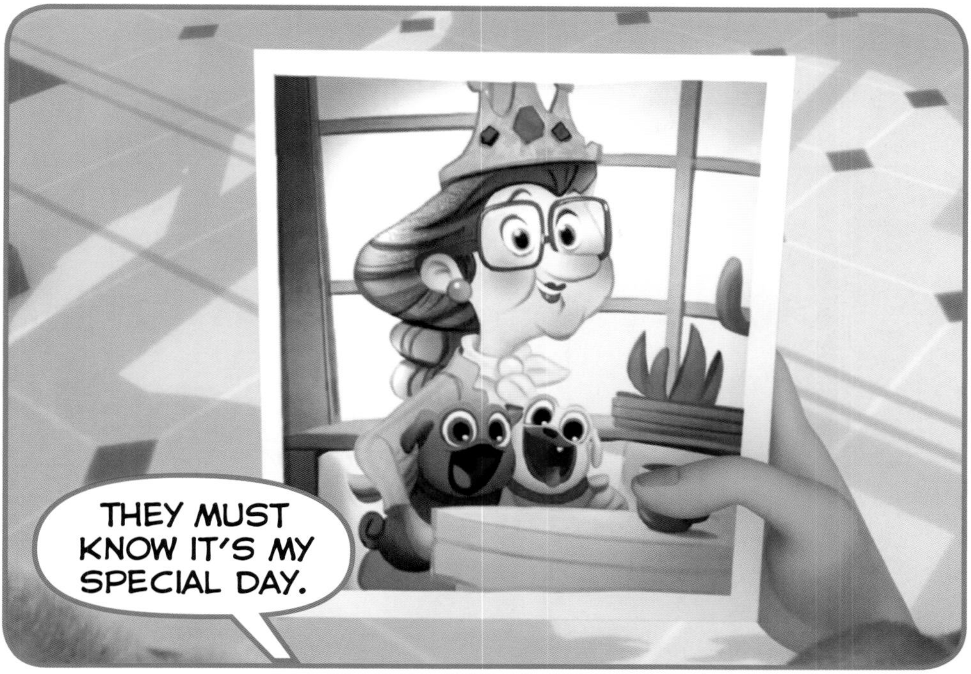
THEY MUST KNOW IT'S MY SPECIAL DAY.

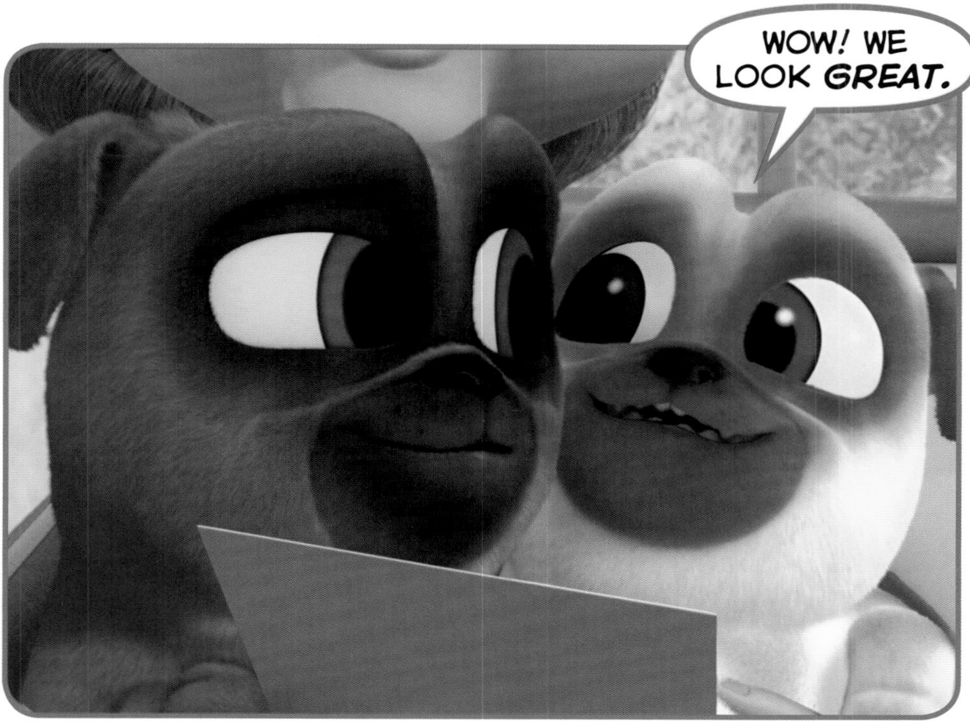
WOW! WE LOOK **GREAT.**

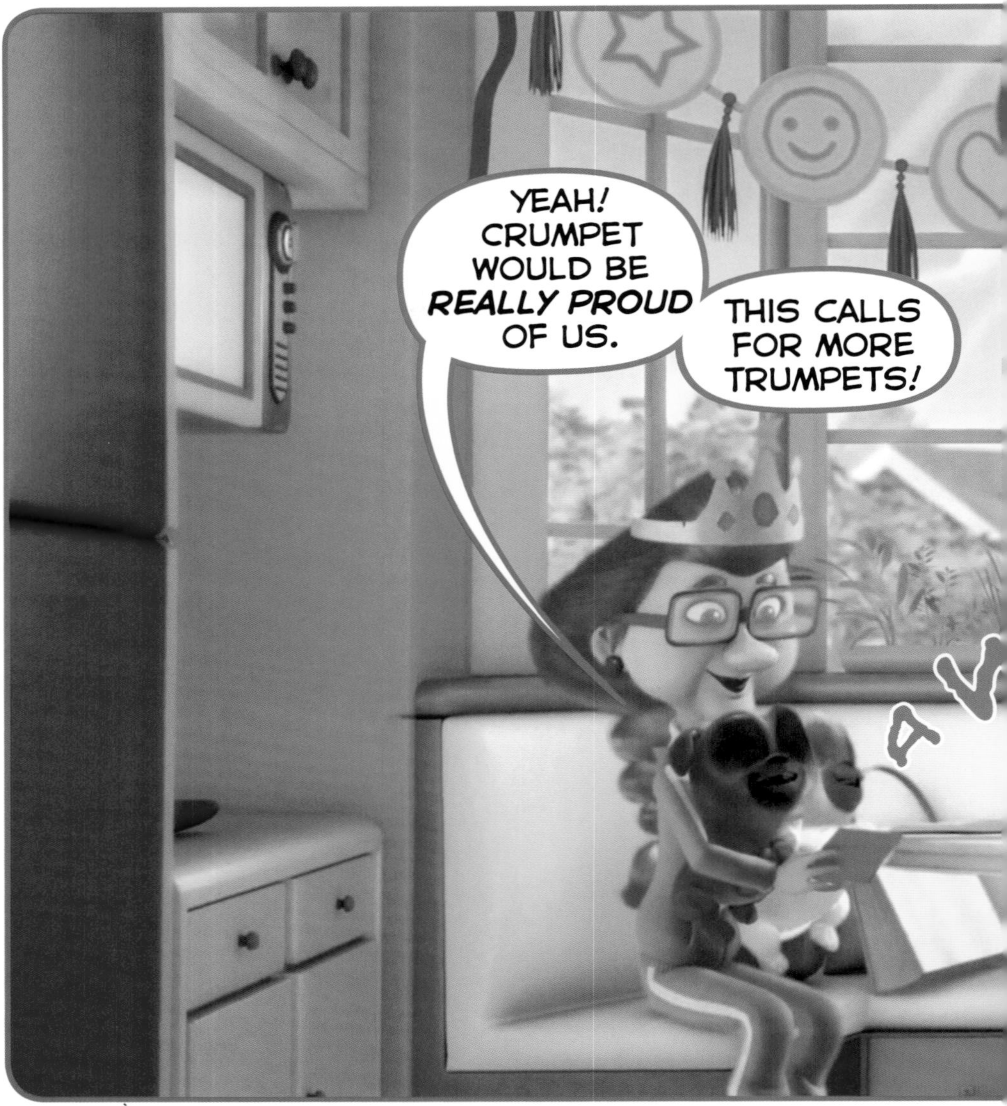
YEAH! CRUMPET WOULD BE REALLY PROUD OF US.
THIS CALLS FOR MORE TRUMPETS!

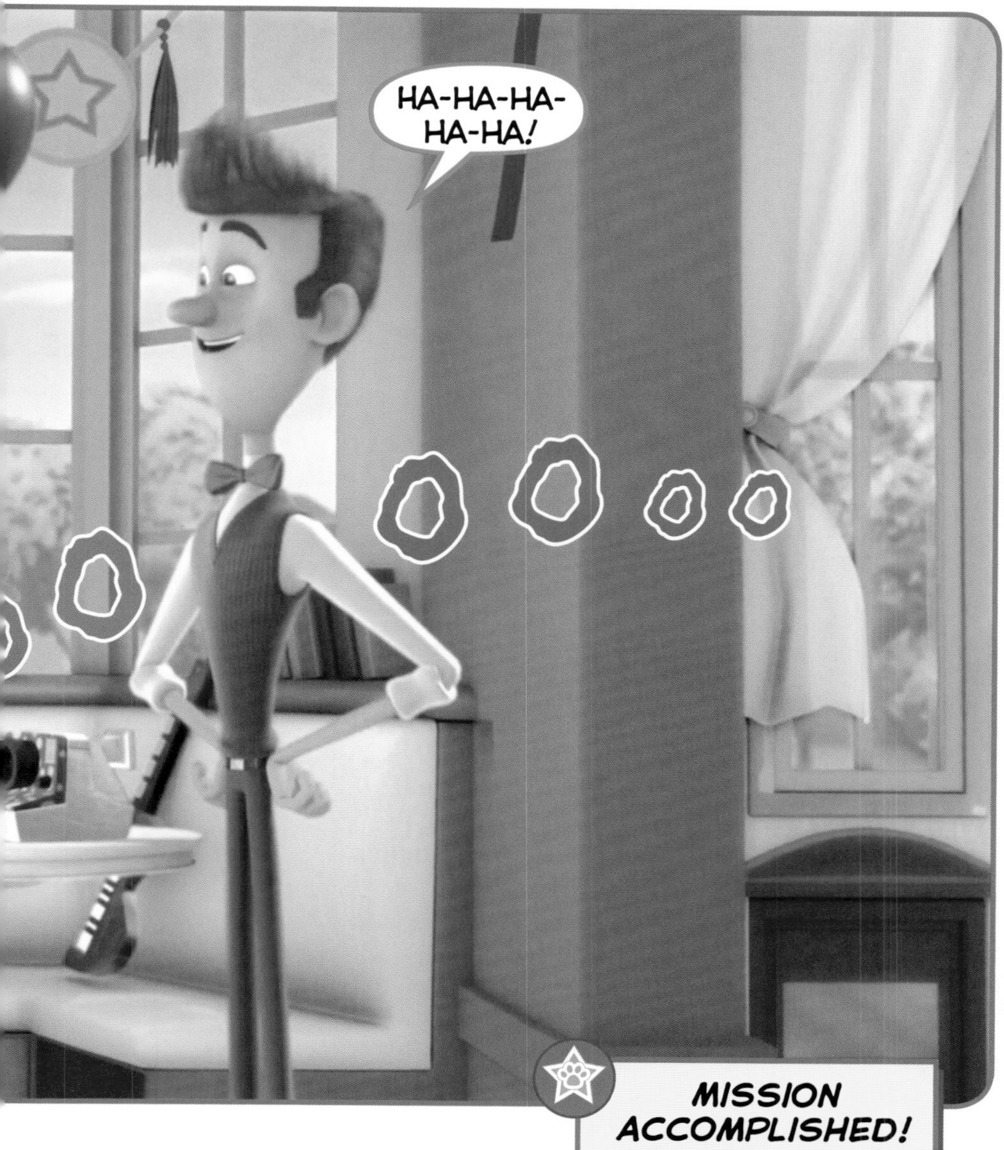
HA-HA-HA-
HA-HA!
MISSION
ACCOMPLISHED!

"Their Royal Pug-ness"

Created by
Harland Williams

Directed by
Stephanie Arnett

Supervising Directors
Trevor Wall
Don MacKinnon

Executive Producers
Sean Coyle
Richard Marlis
Carmen Italia

Written by
Bob Smiley

Storyboard by
Otis Brayboy

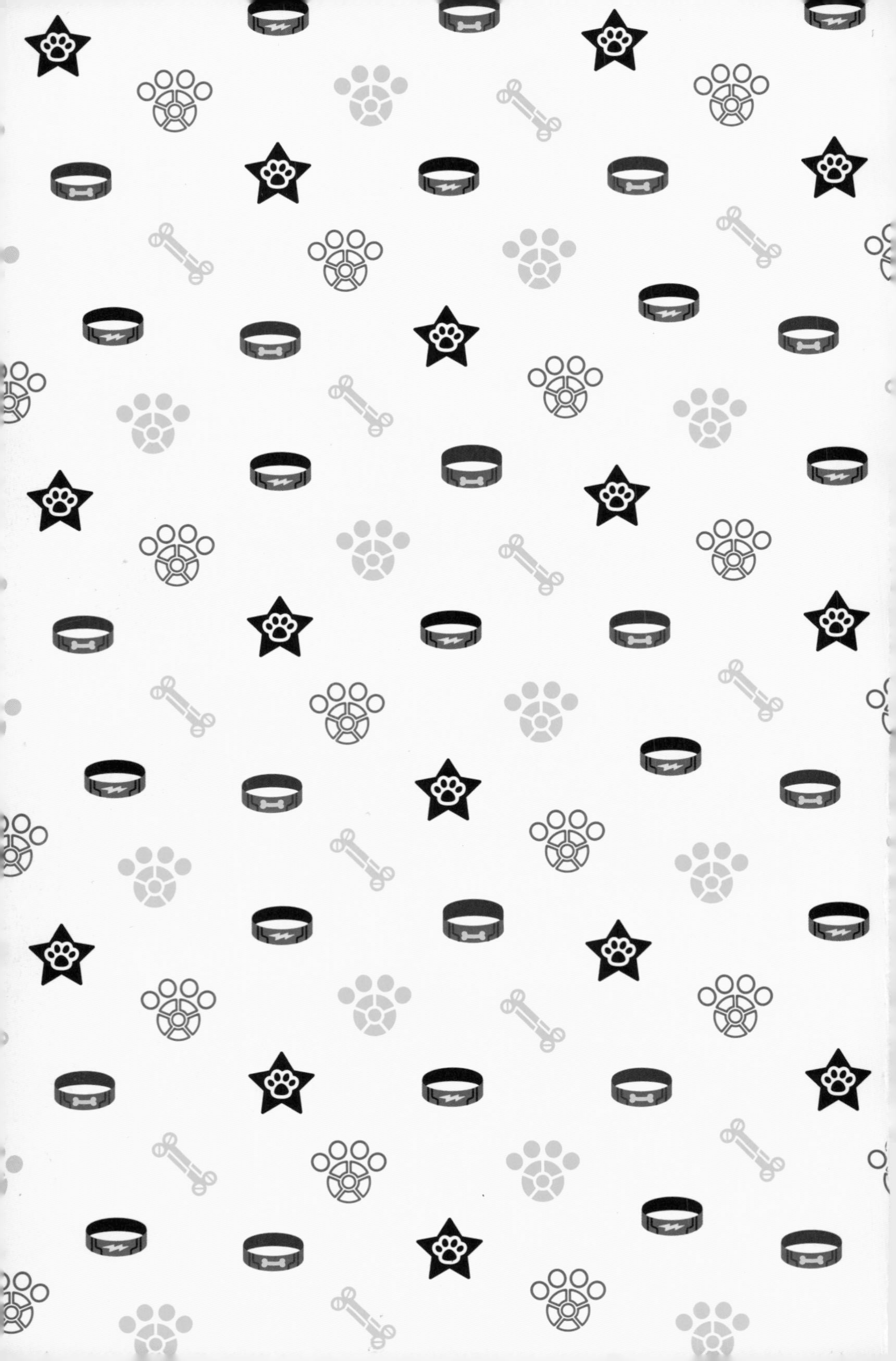

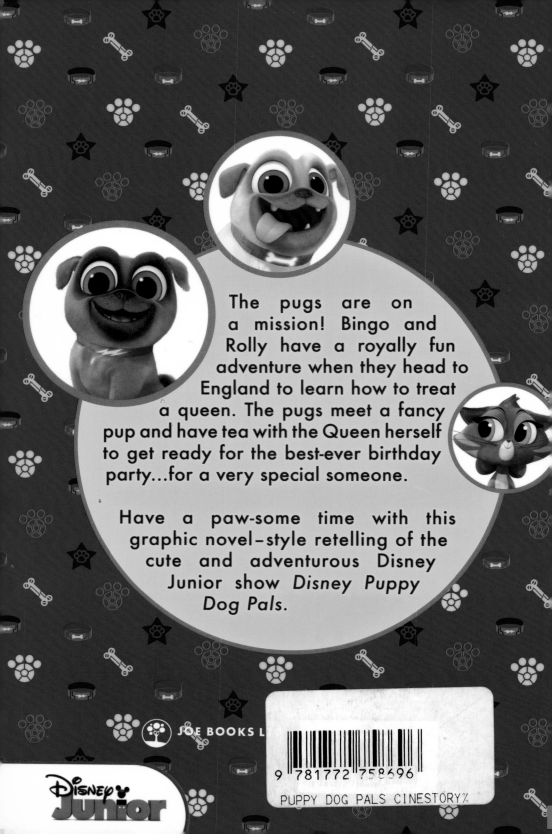

The pugs are on a mission! Bingo and Rolly have a royally fun adventure when they head to England to learn how to treat a queen. The pugs meet a fancy pup and have tea with the Queen herself to get ready for the best-ever birthday party...for a very special someone.

Have a paw-some time with this graphic novel–style retelling of the cute and adventurous Disney Junior show *Disney Puppy Dog Pals*.

JOE BOOKS L

PUPPY DOG PALS CINESTORY%

Disney Junior